GEORGES SIMENON

# MAIGRET'S MEMOIRS

*Translated from the French*

*by*

JEAN STEWART

## HAMISH HAMILTON
LONDON

First published in Great Britain in 1963
by Hamish Hamilton Ltd
90 Great Russell Street, London W.C.1

Copyright © 1950 by Georges Simenon
Translation copyright © 1963 by Hamish Hamilton Ltd

*Maigret's Memoirs (Les Mémoires de Maigret)*
was first published in France in 1950

0856170666

PRINTED AND BOUND IN ENGLAND BY
HAZELL WATSON AND VINEY LTD
AYLESBURY AND SLOUGH

# MAIGRET'S MEMOIRS

This is Maigret's own story. We catch a glimpse of his childhood, we learn of the reasons for his decision to become a policeman, we eavesdrop on his first meeting with the pretty, sympathetic girl who is to become his wife. We follow him step by step, as he moves from department to department. We see him pacing up and down the streets, bitterly cold and the rain seeping through the soles of his hobnailed shoes; suffocating in the oppressive heat of the *grands magasins*, while he watches for likely shoplifters; enduring the jeers and the catcalls of the prostitutes, as he goes from seedy hotel to seedy hotel to search the registers and check the passports; shivering in the bleak, draughty spaces of the Gare du Nord, watching for the slightest twitch of fear on a man's face. In short, we are presented with a panorama of the pathos and the humour, the drudgery and the triumph which every policeman experiences.

But, perhaps most important of all, we watch Maigret's meeting and relationship with Simenon himself. And, in this way, we not only see the workings of Maigret's mind; we also catch a fascinating glimpse of how Simenon started to write his novels and how much Maigret approved or disapproved of the liberties taken with his character and the episodes in his career. For once, we really find out what a character thinks of the author who has written about him.

# CONTENTS

# CHAPTER ONE

*Which affords me a welcome opportunity of explaining
my relations with Monsieur Simenon.*

IT was in 1927 or 1928. I have no memory for dates and
I am not one of those who keep a careful record of their
doings, a habit which is not uncommon in our profession
and which has proved of considerable use and even profit
to some people. And it was only quite recently that I
remembered the notebooks in which my wife, for a long
time without my knowledge and indeed behind my back,
had stuck any newspaper articles that referred to me.

Because of a certain case that gave us some trouble that
year – I could probably discover the exact date, but I
haven't the courage to go and look through those notebooks.

It doesn't matter. At any rate I remember quite clearly
what the weather was like. It was a nondescript day at
the beginning of winter, one of those colourless grey and
white days that I am tempted to call an administrative
day, because one has the impression that nothing interesting can happen in so drab an atmosphere, while in the
office, out of sheer boredom, one feels an urge to bring
one's files up to date, to deal with reports that have been
lying about a long time, to tackle current business fero-
ciously but without zest.

If I stress the unrelieved greyness of the day it is not

from any desire to be picturesque, but in order to show how commonplace the incident itself was, swamped in the trivial happenings of a commonplace day.

It was about ten o'clock in the morning. We had finished making our reports about half an hour ago, for the conference had been short.

Nowadays even the least well-informed members of the public know more or less what's involved in the conferences at Police Headquarters, but in those days most Parisians would have found it hard to say even which Government Service was housed in the Quai des Orfèvres.

At nine o'clock sharp a bell summons the various heads of departments to the Chief's big office, whose windows overlook the Seine. There is no glamour about these gatherings. You go there smoking your pipe or your cigarette, usually with a file tucked under your arm. The day hasn't got going yet, and is still vaguely redolent, for most people, of café au lait and croissants. You shake hands. You gossip, leisurely, waiting for everybody to turn up.

Then each in turn informs the Chief about what has been happening in his sector. A few remain standing, sometimes looking out of the window to watch the buses and taxis crossing the Pont Saint-Michel.

Contrary to general belief, we don't talk exclusively about crime.

'How's your daughter, Priollet? her measles?'

I remember hearing cookery recipes being knowledgeably set forth.

More serious problems are also discussed, of course;

for instance, that of some deputy's or minister's son who has been behaving foolishly, who wilfully persists in his folly, and whom it is imperative to bring back to his senses without causing a scandal. Or that of a rich foreigner who has recently taken up residence in some Grand Hotel in the Champs-Elysées, and about whom the Government has begun to worry. Or of a little girl picked up in the street a few days previously, whom no relative has claimed, although her photograph has appeared in all the newspapers.

This is a gathering of professional people, and events are considered from a strictly professional point of view, without useless talk, so that everything becomes very simple. It's all in the day's work, so to speak.

'Well then, Maigret, haven't you arrested your Pole in the Rue de Birague yet?'

Let me hasten to say that I've nothing against Poles as such. If I happen to speak of them fairly often, it's not that I consider them a particularly aggressive or delinquent set of people. The fact is merely that at that time France, being short of labour-power, imported Poles by the thousand and settled them in the mines in the North. They were collected haphazardly in their own country, whole villages at a time, men, women and children, and piled into trains rather as negro labour was once recruited.

The majority of them have proved to be first class workers, and many of them have become respected citizens. Nevertheless there was a certain proportion of riff-raff, as was only to be expected, and for some time this riffraff gave us a good deal of trouble.

I am trying to convey the atmosphere to the reader by talking thus, somewhat disconnectedly, about the things that were preoccupying me at that time.

'I should like to keep him on the run for two or three days longer, Chief. So far he's led us nowhere. He's sure to end up by meeting some accomplices.'

'The Minister's getting impatient because of the Press . . .'

Always the Press! And always, among the powers that be, that dread of the Press, of public opinion. No sooner has a crime been committed than we are urged to find a culprit immediately, at all costs.

We are practically told, after a few days: 'Put somebody or other in jail in the meantime, just to satisfy public opinion.'

I shall probably revert to this point. In any case it was not the Pole that we were discussing that morning, but a burglary that had recently been committed according to a new technique, which is an uncommon thing.

Three days earlier, on the Boulevard Saint-Denis, in the middle of the day, just as most of the shops had closed for the lunch-hour, a van had stopped in front of a small jeweller's. Some men had unloaded an enormous packing-case, which they had put down close to the door, and had gone off again with the van.

Hundreds of people had passed in front of that case without thinking twice about it. As for the jeweller, when he came back from the restaurant where he had been lunching, he knit puzzled brows.

And when he had shifted the case, which had now become very light, he discovered that a hole had been cut in the side that touched the door, and another hole in the door itself, and that of course all his shelves had been ransacked and his safe as well.

This was the sort of unsensational enquiry that is liable to take months and requires the largest number of men. The burglars had not left a single fingerprint, nor any compromising object.

The fact that the method was a new one made it impossible for us to hunt in any known category of thieves.

We had nothing but the packing-case, an ordinary case although a very large one, and for the past three days a round dozen of detectives had been visiting all manufacturers of packing-cases, and all firms making use of the largest size of packing-case.

I had just returned to my office, where I had begun to draw up a report, when the house telephone rang.

'Is that you, Maigret? Will you come to my room for a moment?'

Nothing surprising about that either. Every day, or almost every day, the Big Chief used to send for me at least once to his office, apart from the conference; I had known him since my childhood, he had often spent his holidays close to our home in the Allier, and he had been a friend of my father's.

And this particular Chief was, in my eyes, the real Chief

in the fullest sense of the word, the chief under whom I had served my first term at Police Headquarters, who, without actually protecting me, had kept a discreet eye on me from above, and whom I had watched, in his black coat and bowler hat, walking alone under fire towards the door of the house in which Bonnot and his gang had for two days been resisting police and gendarmes.

I am referring to Xavier Guichard, with his mischievous eyes and his white hair, as long as a poet's.

'Come in, Maigret.'

The daylight was so dull that morning that the lamp in its green shade was alight on his desk. Close by, in an armchair, I saw a young man who rose to offer me his hand when we were introduced to one another.

'Chief-Inspector Maigret. Monsieur Georges Sim, who's a journalist. . . .'

'Not a journalist, a novelist,' the young man protested smilingly.

Xavier Guichard smiled too. And he had a whole range of smiles which could express all the various shades of what he was thinking. He also had at his disposal a sort of irony, perceptible only to those who knew him well and which, to others, sometimes made him appear a simpleton.

He spoke to me with the utmost seriousness, as if we were concerned with an important affair, a prominent personality.

'For his novel-writing, Monsieur Sim needs to know how Headquarters functions. As he has just explained to me, a good many dramatic stories wind up in this house.

He has also made it clear that it's not so much the workings of the police machine that he wants to study in detail, for he has been able to get information about these elsewhere, but rather the atmosphere in which these operations take place.'

I merely glanced at the young man, who must have been about twenty-four and who was thin, with hair almost as long as the Chief's, and of whom the least I can say is that he seemed to have no lack of confidence about anything, least of all about himself.

'Will you show him round, Maigret?'

And just as I was moving towards the door I heard the fellow Sim remark:

'Excuse me, Monsieur Guichard, but you've forgotten to mention to the Chief-Inspector . . .'

'Oh yes, you're quite right. Monsieur Sim, as he has reminded us, is not a journalist. So there's no danger of his reporting to the newspapers things that ought to remain unpublished. He has promised me, without being asked, to use only in his novels whatever he may see or hear amongst us, and that in a form sufficiently altered to create no difficulties for us.'

I can still hear the Chief adding gravely, as he bent forward to look at his mail:

'You needn't worry, Maigret. He has given me his word.'

All the same, Xavier Guichard had let himself be led astray, I felt that already and my feeling was subsequently confirmed. Not only by the youthful audacity of his visitor, but on account of something that I only discovered later. The Chief, apart from his profession, had one passion : archaeology. He belonged to several learned societies and had written a fat book (which I have never read) about the remote origins of Paris and its surroundings.

Now young Sim had discovered this, whether or not by chance, and had made a point of talking to him about it.

Was it on this account that I had been sent for personally ? Almost every day somebody at Headquarters gets the job of showing round visitors. Generally these are distinguished foreigners, or those connected in some way with the police force of their country, or sometimes merely influential voters, come up from the provinces and proudly exhibiting a card from their Deputy. It has become a routine. There is practically a little lecture that everybody has more or less learnt by heart, like guides to historical monuments.

But usually a sergeant serves the purpose, and the visitor has to be somebody very important for the head of a department to be disturbed.

'If you like,' I proposed, 'we'll go first to the anthropometrical department.'

'If it isn't too much bother, I'd rather begin with the waiting-room.'

This was my first surprise. He said it quite nicely, too, with a disarming glance, explaining :

'You understand, I should like to follow the route that your clients usually follow.'

'In that case you ought to start at the Police Station, for most of them spend the night there before being brought to us.'

He replied, calmly:

'I visited the Police Station last night.'

He took no notes. He had neither notebook nor fountain pen. He stayed for several minutes in the waiting-room with its tall windows, where are displayed, in black frames, the photographs of members of the Force killed on duty.

'How many casualties each year, on an average?'

Then he asked to see my office. Now it so happened that at that period the workmen were busy refitting it. I was provisionally installed on the mezzanine, in a disused office in the oldest administrative style, thick with dust, with black wooden furniture and a coal-burning stove of the sort you can still see in certain provincial railway stations.

This was the office in which I had started my professional life, in which I had worked as Detective-Sergeant for some fifteen years, and I must admit that I harboured a certain fondness for that huge stove, whose iron bars I loved to see glowing red in winter, and which I used to stoke up to the brim. This was not so much an inveterate habit as a trick to keep myself in countenance. In the middle of a difficult interrogation I would get up and poke the fire lengthily, then throw in noisy shovelfuls of coal, looking quite bland, while my client stared at me in bewilderment.

And the fact is that when at last I had a modern office at my disposal, equipped with central heating, I missed my old stove, but I was never allowed, nor ever even made the request – which would not have been granted – to take it with me into my new premises.

I must apologise for lingering over these details, but I know more or less what I'm getting at.

My guest looked at my pipes, my ashtrays, the black marble clock on the chimney-piece, the little enamel basin behind the door, and the towel that always smells like a wet dog.

He asked me no technical questions. The files did not seem to interest him in the slightest.

'This staircase takes us to the laboratory.'

There, too, he stared at the ceiling, which was partly glazed, at the walls, at the floor, and at the dummy which is used for certain reconstructions, but he paid no attention either to the laboratory itself with its complicated apparatus or to the work which was going on there.

Out of habit, I tried to explain :

'By magnifying several hundred times any written text, and comparing it . . .'

'I know. I know.'

And then he asked me, casually :

'Have you read Hans Gross?'

I had never heard the name mentioned. I have since learnt that it was that of an Austrian magistrate who, in the 1880's, held the first chair of scientific criminology at the University of Vienna.

My visitor, however, had read Hans Gross's two fat volumes. He had read everything, quantities of books of whose very existence I was ignorant and whose titles he quoted at me in an offhand manner.

'Follow me along this passage, and I'll show you the Records Office, where we keep the files of . . .'

'I know. I know.'

I was beginning to find him irritating. It looked as if he had put me to all this bother solely in order to stare at walls and ceilings and floors, to stare at us all, as if he were drawing up an inventory.

'We shall find a crowd in the anthropometric department just now. They'll have finished with the women by now. It'll be the men's turn . . .'

There were some twenty of these, stark naked, who had been rounded up during the night, and were waiting their turn to be measured and photographed.

'In short,' the young man said to me, 'all I've still got to see is the Special Infirmary of the Police Station.'

I frowned.

'Visitors are not admitted.'

It is one of the least-known places, where criminals and suspects are put through a number of mental tests by police doctors.

'Paul Bourget used to watch the proceedings,' my visitor calmly replied. 'I shall ask for permission.'

The fact is that I retained a wholly uninteresting memory of him, as uninteresting as the weather itself that day. If I made no effort to cut short his visit, it was primarily on account of the Chief's recommendation, and also because I had nothing important to do, and that it was, after all, a way of killing time.

He happened to pass through my office again, sat down and held out his tobacco pouch to me.

'I see you're a pipe smoker too. I like pipe smokers.'

There were, as usual, a good half dozen pipes lying about, and he examined them with a connoisseur's eye.

'What case are you on at the moment?'

In my most professional tone I told him about the robbery where the packing-case had been left at the door of the jeweller's shop, pointing out that this was the first time this technique had been used.

'No,' he said to me. 'It was used eight years ago in New York, at a shop in Eighth Avenue.'

He must have been pleased with himself, but I must admit that he did not seem to be boasting. He was smoking his pipe gravely, as if to add ten years to his age and put himself on an equal footing with the mature man that I already was.

'You see, Chief-Inspector, I'm not interested in professionals. Their psychology offers no problems. They are just men doing their own job, and that's all.'

'What are you interested in?'

'The others. Those who are made like you or me, and who end up one fine day by killing somebody without being prepared to do so.'

'There are very few of those.'

'I know.'

'Apart from crimes of passion . . .'

'There's nothing interesting about them either.'

That's all I remember of that encounter. I must have spoken to him incidentally of a case on which I had been busy a few months earlier, just because professionals were not involved in it, a case concerning a young girl and a pearl necklace.

'Thank you, Chief-Inspector. I hope I shall have the pleasure of meeting you again.'

Privately, I said to myself : 'I sincerely hope not.'

.    .    .

Weeks passed, then months. Once in the middle of winter I thought I recognised the fellow Sim in the main corridor of Police Headquarters, pacing up and down.

One morning I found on my desk, beside my mail, a little book in a revolting illustrated cover, such as are displayed on newspaper stalls and read by shop girls. It was called : *The Girl with the Pearl Necklace*, and the author was called Georges Sim.

I hadn't even the curiosity to read it. I read few books, and no popular novels. I don't even know where I put the book, a paperback printed on cheap paper, probably in the wastepaper basket, and I thought no more about it for several days.

Then one morning I found an identical book in the same place on my desk, and thenceforward each morning a fresh copy appeared beside my mail.

It was some time before I noticed that my Inspectors, particularly Lucas, were glancing at me with amusement.

At last Lucas said to me, after beating about the bush for a long time, as we made our way to the Brasserie Dauphine one day for a drink before lunch :

'So you're a character in a novel now, Chief.'

He pulled the book out of his pocket.

'Have you read it ?'

He confessed that it was Janvier, the youngest member of the squad at that time, who had been putting a copy of the book on my desk each morning.

'It's quite like you in some ways, you'll see.'

He was right. It was like me to the extent that a sketch scribbled on the marble top of a café table by an amateur caricaturist is like a flesh-and-blood human being.

It made me bigger and clumsier than life, peculiarly ponderous, so to speak.

As for the story, it was unrecognisable, and I was made to use some quite unexpected methods, to say the least.

That same evening I found my wife with the book in her hands.

'The woman in the dairy gave it me. Apparently it's about you. I haven't had time to read it yet.'

What could I do? As the man Sim had promised, no newspaper was involved. The book concerned was not a serious work, but a cheap publication to which it would have been absurd to attach any importance.

He had used my real name. But he might have replied that there are quite a number of Maigrets in the world. I merely promised myself to receive him somewhat coldly if I happened to meet him again, convinced meanwhile that he would avoid setting foot in Police Headquarters.

In which I was mistaken. One day when I knocked at the Chief's door without having been sent for, to ask his advice on some point, he said :

'Come in, Maigret. I was just going to call you. Our friend Sim is here.'

No signs of embarrassment about our friend Sim. On the contrary, complete self-confidence and a bigger pipe than ever in his mouth.

'How are you, Chief-Inspector ?'

And Guichard explained :

'He's just been reading me a few passages from something he has written about our place.'

'I know about it.'

Xavier Guichard's eyes were full of laughter, but this time it was of me that he seemed to be making fun.

'Then he told me some rather relevant things which may interest you. He'll repeat them to you.'

'It's quite simple. Hitherto, in France, in books, with very few exceptions, the sympathetic character has always been the offender, while the police has been exposed to ridicule, if not worse.'

Guichard was nodding approvingly.

'Quite true, isn't it ?'

And it was, in fact, quite true. Not only in books but in daily life. I was reminded of a rather painful episode in my early days, when I was serving in the Public Highways Squad. I was on the point of arresting a pickpocket outside a Metro station when the fellow began yelling something – possibly 'Stop thief!'

Instantly a score of people fell upon me. I explained to them that I was a policeman, that the man now making his escape was a habitual criminal. I am convinced that they all believed me. They nonetheless managed to delay me by every possible means, thus allowing my pickpocket time to get away.

'Well,' Guichard went on, 'our friend Sim is proposing to write a series of novels in which the police will be shown in its true light.'

I pulled a face, which the Chief did not fail to notice.

'More or less in its true light,' he corrected himself. 'You follow me? His book is only a rough draft of what he plans to do.'

'He has made use of my name.'

I thought the young man would be covered with confusion and would apologise. Not a bit of it.

'I hope you weren't offended, Chief-Inspector. I couldn't help it. When I have imagined a character under a particular name I find it quite impossible to change it. I tried out all possible combinations of syllables to replace those of the name Maigret, but in vain. In the end I gave it up. It wouldn't have been *my* character any longer.'

He said *my* character, quite calmly, and the amazing thing was that I never turned a hair, possibly on account of Xavier Guichard and the mischievously twinkling eyes he kept fixed on me.

'He is thinking this time not of a popular series but of

what he calls ... What did you call it, Monsieur Sim?'

'Semi-literature.'

'And you're counting on me to ...'

'I should like to know you better.'

I told you at the beginning: his self-assurance was complete. I really believe that was the secret of his strength. It was partly through this that he had already succeeded in winning over the Chief, who was interested in every type of human being and who announced to me, without a smile:

'He is only twenty-four.'

'I find it hard to construct a character unless I know how he behaves at every moment of the day. For instance, I shan't be able to talk about millionaires until I have seen one in his dressing-gown eating his boiled egg for breakfast.'

This happened a long time ago and I wonder now for what mysterious reason we listened to all this without bursting out laughing.

'In short you'd like ...'

'To know you better, to watch you living and working.'

Of course, the Chief gave me no orders. I should no doubt have rebelled. For quite a time I felt uncertain whether he wasn't playing a practical joke on me, for he had retained a certain Latin Quarter streak in his character, from the days when the Latin Quarter still went in for hoaxes.

It was probably in order not to seem to be taking the

whole affair too seriously that I said, shrugging my shoulders :

'Whenever you like.'

Then young Sim jumped up delightedly.

'Right away.'

Once more, in retrospect, it may seem ridiculous. The dollar was worth I don't know what fantastic sums. Americans used to light their cigars with thousand-franc notes. Montmartre was teeming with negro musicians, and rich, middle-aged ladies let themselves be robbed of their jewellery by Argentinian gigolos at *thés dansants*.

The sale of *La Garçonne* was reaching astronomical figures, and the Vice Squad was overwhelmed by orgiastic parties in the Bois de Boulogne, which they scarcely dared interrupt for fear of disturbing Consular personalities having their fun.

Women had short hair and short skirts, and men wore pointed shoes and trousers tight round the ankles.

This explains nothing, I know. But everything is interconnected. And I can still see young Sim coming into my office next morning, as if he were one of my inspectors, remarking kindly : 'Don't let me disturb you . . .' and going to sit down in a corner.

He still took no notes. He asked few questions. He tended rather to make assertions. He explained to me subsequently — and it doesn't follow that I believed him — that a man's reactions to an assertion are more revealing than his replies to a specific question.

One day at noon when we went for a drink to the

Brasserie Dauphine, Lucas, Janvier and I, as was our frequent custom, he followed us.

And one morning, at the conference, I found him installed in a corner of the Chief's office.

This went on for several months. When I asked him if he was writing, he answered :

'Popular novels, still, to earn my living. From four to eight in the morning. By eight o'clock I've finished my day's work. I shall only start on semi-literary novels when I feel ready for it.'

I don't know what he meant by that, but, after I had invited him to lunch one Sunday in the Boulevard Richard-Lenoir and had introduced him to my wife, he suddenly stopped coming to the Quai des Orfèvres.

It seemed odd not to see him in his corner, getting up when I got up, following me when I went out and accompanying me step by step through the offices.

During that spring I received an invitation that was, to say the least, unexpected.

*Georges Sim has the honour of inviting you to the christening of his boat, the* Ostrogoth, *which will be performed by the Curé of Notre-Dame on Tuesday next, at the Spanish du Vert-Galant.*

I did not go. I learnt from the police of the district that for three days and three nights a rowdy gang kept up a tremendous din on board a boat moored right in the middle of Paris and flying all its flags.

Once, as I crossed the Pont-Neuf, I saw the aforesaid

boat and, at the foot of the mast, somebody sitting at a typewriter, wearing a master-mariner's cap.

The following week the boat had gone, and the Square du Vert-Galant had resumed its usual appearance.

More than a year later I received another invitation, written this time on one of our fingerprint cards.

*Georges Simenon has the honour of inviting you to the Anthropometrical Ball which will be held at the* Boule Blanche *to celebrate the launching of his detective stories.*

Sim had turned into Simenon.

More precisely, feeling himself now fully adult, perhaps, he had resumed his real name.

I did not bother about it. I did not go to the ball in question and I learned next day that the Prefect of Police had been present.

Through the newspapers. The same newspapers that informed me, on the front page, that Chief-Inspector Maigret had just made his sensational entry into detective fiction.

That morning, when I arrived at Headquarters and climbed the great staircase, I was met with sly smiles and amused averted faces.

My inspectors did their utmost to keep straight faces. My colleagues, at the conference, pretended to treat me with unwonted respect.

Only the Big Chief behaved as if nothing had happened and asked me with an absent-minded air :

'And what about you, Maigret? How are things going?'

In the shops of the Richard-Lenoir district, there was not a tradesman who failed to show my wife the paper with my name in large letters, and ask her, full of wonderment:

'It *is* your husband, isn't it?'

It was myself, alas!

# CHAPTER TWO

*In which it is argued that the naked truth is often
unconvincing and that dressed-up truths may
seem more real than life.*

WHEN the news got round that I was writing this book,
and then that Simenon's publisher, without having read
it, before I had even finished the first chapter, had offered
to publish it, I was conscious of the somewhat dubious
approval of my friends. They were saying, I'm convinced
of it : 'So Maigret's having a go too !'

The fact is that during the last few years, at least three
of my former colleagues, men of my own generation, have
written and published their memoirs.

Let me hasten to point out that in so doing they were
following an old tradition of the Paris police, to which we
owe, among others, the memoirs of Macé and those of the
great Goron, each in his time chief of what was then called
the Sûreté. As for the most illustrious of them all, Vidocq,
he unfortunately left no recollections written by himself
which we might compare with the portraits drawn of him
by novelists, often under his real name, or else, as in the
case of Balzac, under that of Vautrin.

It is not my business to defend my colleagues, but nevertheless I take this opportunity of replying to an objection
which I have frequently heard raised.

'According to their writings,' I have been told, 'at least

28

three of them consider themselves responsible for the solution of every famous case.'

And people would quote, in particular, the Mestorino case, which made a great sensation in its time.

Now I might make a similar claim myself, for a case of that scope demands the collaboration of every branch of the Force. As for the final interrogation, that famous twenty-eight-hour-long interrogation that is cited as an example nowadays, there were not four but at least six of us taking it in shifts, going over the same questions one by one in every conceivable fashion, gaining a little bit of ground each time.

Under these conditions, it would have been hard to say which of us at a given moment had pulled the trigger that provoked a confession.

I wish to assert, moreover, that the title of *Memoirs* was not chosen by myself and was finally tacked on because we couldn't think of a better word.

The same is true (I make this point as I correct the proofs) of the sub-titles, of what it seems are called chapter-headings, which the publisher asked me to let him add as an after-thought, for typographical reasons, he told me kindly; in actual fact, I suppose, to give a touch of lightness to my text.

Of all the tasks I fulfilled at Headquarters, the only one I ever shirked was the writing up of reports. Was this due to an atavistic desire for accuracy, to scruples with which I have seen my father wrestling before me?

The joke has been made so often that it is almost a classic :

'Maigret's reports consist largely of parentheses.'

Probably because I try to explain too much, to explain everything, and because nothing seems to me clear or definite.

If *memoirs* implies the story of the events in which I have been involved in the course of my career, I'm afraid the public will be disappointed.

In the space of almost half a century I don't think there have been more than a score of really sensational cases, including those to which I have already referred : the Bonnot case, the Mestorino case, plus the Landru case, the Sarrat case and a few others.

Now my colleagues, my former chiefs in some cases, have spoken about these at length.

As for the other investigations, those which were interesting in themselves but hit no headlines in the newspapers, Simenon has dealt with them.

This brings me to what I wanted to say, what I've been trying to say ever since I started this manuscript, namely the real justification for these memoirs which are not proper memoirs, and now I know less than ever how I am to express myself.

I once read in the papers that Anatole France, who must at any rate have been an intelligent man and who was fond of indulging in irony, having sat for the painter Van Dongen for his portrait, not only refused to accept the picture once it was finished but forbade it to be shown in public.

It was at about the same period that a famous actress brought a sensational lawsuit against a caricaturist whose portrait of her she thought insulting and injurious to her career.

I am neither an Academician nor a stage star. I don't consider myself unduly susceptible. Never, during the course of my professional life, have I sent any single correction to the newspapers, although these have never been slow to criticise my activities and my methods.

Nowadays everyone cannot have his portrait painted, but at least we have all had the experience of being photographed. And I suppose everyone is familiar with that discomfort we feel when confronted with a picture of ourselves which is not quite a true likeness.

Is my meaning quite clear? I am rather ashamed of insisting on this. I know I am dealing with a vital, ultra-sensitive point, and I feel suddenly afraid of appearing ridiculous, a thing which rarely affects me.

I think I should scarcely mind if I were depicted under an appearance completely different from my own, even libellously so.

But let me revert to the comparison with photography. The lens does not permit of complete inaccuracy. The image is different without being different. Faced with the print, you are frequently incapable of putting your finger on the detail that offends you, of saying exactly *what* isn't you, *what* you don't recognise as belonging to yourself.

Well, for years this was my position when faced with Simenon's Maigret, whom I watched growing day by day beside me, so that some people ended by asking me quite seriously whether I had copied his mannerisms, and others whether my name was really my father's name or whether I had borrowed it from the novelist.

I have tried to explain more or less how the thing began, quite innocently on the whole and seemingly without importance.

The very youthfulness of the fellow whom worthy Xavier Guichard had introduced to me one day in his office inclined me rather to shrug my shoulders than to harbour suspicions.

And then, a few months later, I was properly caught up in a mesh from which I have never managed to escape and from which the pages I am now scribbling will not completely rescue me.

'What are you grumbling about? You're famous!'

I know! I know! It's easy to say that when you've not experienced it. I even admit that at certain moments, in certain circumstances, it's not disagreeable. Not merely because it flatters one's vanity. Often for practical reasons. For instance, merely to secure a good seat in a crowded train or restaurant, or to avoid having to queue.

For so many years I never protested, any more than I corrected misstatements in the newspapers.

And I'm not suddenly going to claim that I was boiling inwardly, or chafing at the bit. That would be exaggerating, and I detest exaggeration.

None the less I promised myself that one day I would say what I've got to say, quite quietly, without rancour or ill-feeling, and once for all put things in their true perspective.

And that day has come.

Why is this book called *Memoirs*? I'm not responsible for that, as I said before, and the word is not of my choosing.

I'm not really concerned here with Mestorino or Landru or with that lawyer in the Massif Central who exterminated his victims by plunging them into a bath full of quicklime.

I'm concerned, more simply, with setting one character against another, one truth against another truth.

.     .     .

You shall soon see what some people understand by truth.

It was at the beginning, at the time of that anthropometrical ball which, together with certain other somewhat spectacular affairs in questionable taste, served to launch what people were already beginning to call 'the first Maigrets', two volumes entitled: *The Hanged Man of Saint-Pholien* and *The Late Monsieur Gallet*.

Those two, I frankly admit, I read immediately. And I can still picture Simenon appearing in my office the next morning, pleased at being himself, even more self-assured than before if that were possible, but none the less with a trace of anxiety in his eyes.

'I know what you're going to say to me!' he flung at me as soon as I opened my mouth.

Pacing up and down, he began to explain :

'I'm quite aware that these books are crammed with technical inaccuracies. There's no need to count them up. Let me tell you they're deliberate, and this is why.'

I didn't take note of the whole of his speech, but I remember the essential point in it, which he often repeated to me subsequently with an almost sadistic pleasure :

'Truth never seems true. I don't mean only in literature or in painting. I won't remind you either of those Doric columns whose lines seem to us strictly perpendicular and which only give that impression because they are slightly curved. If they were straight, they'd look as if they were swelling, don't you see?'

In those days he was still fond of displaying his erudition.

'Tell someone a story, any story. If you don't dress it up, it'll seem incredible, artificial. Dress it up, and it'll seem more real than life.'

He trumpeted out those last words as if they implied some sensational discovery.

'The whole problem is to make something more real than life. Well, I've done that! I've made you more real than life.'

I remained speechless. For a moment I could find nothing to say, poor unreal policeman that I was.

And he proceeded to demonstrate, with an abundance of gestures and the hint of a Belgian accent, that my investigations as told by him were more convincing – he may even have said more accurate – than as experienced by myself.

At the time of our first encounters, in the autumn, he had not been lacking in self-confidence. Thanks to success, he was brimming over with it now, he had enough to spare for all the timid folk on earth.

'Follow me carefully, Inspector . . .'

For he had decided to drop the *monsieur le commissaire.*

'In a real investigation there are fifty of you, if not more, busy hunting for the criminal. You and your detectives aren't alone on the trail. The police and gendarmerie of the whole country are on the alert. They are busy in railway stations and ports and at frontiers. Not to mention the informers, let alone all the amateurs who take a hand.

'Just try, in the two hundred or two hundred and fifty pages of a novel to give a tolerably faithful picture of that swarming activity! A three-decker novel wouldn't be long enough, and the reader would lose heart after a few chapters, muddling everything, confusing everything.

'Now who is it that in real life prevents this confusion from taking place, who is there every morning putting everyone in his right place and following the guiding thread?'

He looked me up and down triumphantly.

'It's you yourself, as you know very well. It's the man in charge of the investigation. I'm quite aware that a

Chief-Inspector from Central Police Headquarters, the head of a special squad, doesn't roam the streets in person to interview concierges and wine merchants.

'I'm quite aware, too, that, apart from exceptional cases, you don't spend your nights tramping about in the rain in empty streets waiting for some window to light up or some door to open.

'None the less things happen exactly as if you were there yourself, isn't that so?'

What could I reply to this? From a certain point of view it was a logical conclusion.

'So then, let's simplify! The first quality, the essential quality of truth is to be simple. And I have simplified. I have reduced to their simplest form the wheels within wheels that surround you, without altering the result in the slightest.

'Where fifty more or less anonymous detectives were swarming in confusion, I have retained only three or four, each with his own personality.'

I tried to object:

'The rest won't like it.'

'I don't write for a few dozen police officials. When you write a book about schoolmasters you're bound to offend tens of thousands of schoolmasters. The same would happen if you wrote about station-masters or typists. What were we talking about?'

'The different sorts of truth.'

'I was trying to prove to you that my sort is the only valid one. Would you like another example? One doesn't

36

need to have spent as long as I have in this building to know that Central Police Headquarters, which belongs to the Prefecture of Police, can only operate within the perimeter of Paris and, by extension, in certain cases, within the Department of the Seine.

'Now in *The Late Monsieur Gallet* I described an investigation which took place in the centre of France.

'Did you go there, yes or no?'

It was yes, of course.

'I went there, it's true, but at a period when . . .'

'At a period when, for a certain length of time, you were working not for the Quai des Orfèvres but for the Rue des Saussaies. Why bother the reader's head with these administrative subtleties?

'Must one begin the account of every case by explaining: This took place in such and such a year. So Maigret was seconded to such and such a department.'

'Let me finish . . .'

He had his idea and knew that he was about to touch a weak point.

'Are you, in your habits, your attitude, your character, a Quai des Orfèvres man or a Rue des Saussaies man?'

I apologise to my colleagues of the Sûreté Nationale, who include many of my good friends, but I am divulging no secret when I admit that there is, to say the least, a certain rivalry between the two establishments.

Let us admit, too, as Simenon had understood from the beginning, that, particularly in those days, there existed two rather different types of policeman.

Those of the Rue des Saussaies, who are directly answerable to the Ministry of the Interior, are led more or less inevitably to deal with political jobs.

I don't blame them for it. I simply confess that for my own part I'd rather not be responsible for these.

Our field of action at the Quai des Orfèvres is perhaps more restricted, more down to earth. Our job, in fact, is to cope with malefactors of every sort and, in general, with everything that comes under the heading 'police' with the specific limitation 'judiciary'.

'You'll grant me that you're a Quai des Orfèvres man. You're proud of it. Well, that's what I've made of you; I've tried to make you the incarnation of a Quai des Orfèvres man. And now, for the sake of minutiae, because of your mania for accuracy, have I got to spoil the clarity of the picture by explaining that in such and such a year, for certain complex reasons, you provisionally changed your department, which enabled you to work in any part of France?'

'But . . .'

'One moment. The first day I met you, I told you I was not a journalist but a novelist, and I remember promising Monsieur Guichard that my stories would never involve indiscretions that might prove awkward for the Police.'

'I know, but . . .'

'Wait a minute, Maigret, for God's sake!'

It was the first time he had called me that. It was the first time, too, that this youngster had told me to shut up.

'I've changed the names, except for yours and those of

two or three of your colleagues. I've been careful to change the place-names too. Often, for an extra precaution, I've changed the family relationship between the characters.

'I have simplified things, and sometimes I've described only one cross-examination where there were really four or five, and only two or three trails to be followed where, to begin with, you had ten in front of you.

'I maintain that I am in the right, that my truth is the right one.

'I've brought you a proof of it.'

He pointed to a pile of books which he had laid on my desk when he arrived and to which I had paid no attention.

'These are the books written by specialists on matters concerning the police during the last twenty years, true stories, of that sort of truth that you like.

'Read them. For the most part you're familiar with the investigations which these books describe in detail.

'Well! I'm willing to bet that you won't recognise them, precisely because the quest for objectivity falsifies that truth which always is and which always *must* be simple.

'And now . . .'

Well! I'd rather admit it right away. That was the moment when I realised where the shoe pinched.

He was quite right, dammit, on all the heads he had mentioned. I didn't worry in the least, either, because he'd reduced the number of detectives or made me spend nights in the rain in their stead, or because he had, deliberately or not, confused the Sûreté Nationale with Central Police Headquarters.

What shocked me, actually, although I scarcely liked to admit it to myself, was ...

Good Lord, how hard this is! Remember what I said about a man and his photograph.

To take merely the detail of the bowler hat. I may appear quite ridiculous, but I must confess that this silly detail hurt me more than all the rest.

When young Sim came to Headquarters for the first time, I still had a bowler hat in my cupboard, but I only wore it on rare occasions, for funerals or official ceremonies.

Now it happened that in my office there hung a photograph taken some years earlier on the occasion of some congress or other, in which I appeared wearing that cursed hat.

The result is that even today, when I am introduced to people who've never seen me before, I hear them say:

'Why, you're wearing a different hat.'

As for the famous overcoat with the velvet collar, it was with my wife that Simenon had to have it out one day, rather than with myself.

I did have such a coat, I admit. I even had several, like all men of my generation. It may even have happened that, round about 1927, on a day of extreme cold or driving rain, I took down one of those old overcoats.

I'm not a dressy man. I care very little about being smart. But perhaps for that very reason I've a horror of looking odd. And my little Jewish tailor in the Rue de Turenne is no more anxious than I am to have me stared at in the street.

'Is it my fault if that's how I see you?' Simenon might have answered, like the painter who gives his model a crooked nose or a squint.

Only in that case the model doesn't have to spend his whole life in front of his portrait, and thousands of people aren't going to believe ever after that he has a crooked nose or a squint.

I didn't tell him all this that morning. I merely averted my eyes and said modestly :

'Was it absolutely necessary to simplify *me*?'

'To begin with, it certainly was. The public has to get used to you, to your figure, your bearing. I've probably hit on the right expression. For the moment you're still only a silhouette, a back, a pipe, a way of talking, of muttering.'

'Thanks!'

'The details will appear gradually, you'll see. I don't know how long it will take. Little by little you'll begin to live with a more subtle, more complex life.'

'That's reassuring.'

'For instance, up till now, you've had no family life, whereas the Boulevard Richard-Lenoir and Madame Maigret actually take up a good half of your existence. You've still only rung up your home, but you're going to be seen there.'

'In my dressing-gown and slippers?'

'And even in bed.'

'I wear nightshirts,' I said ironically.

'I know. That completes the picture. Even if you were used to pyjamas I'd have made you wear a nightshirt.'

I wonder how this conversation would have ended – probably with a regular quarrel – if I hadn't been told that a young informer from the Rue Pigalle wanted to speak to me.

'On the whole,' I said to Simenon, as he held out his hand, 'you're pleased with yourself.'

'Not yet, but it'll come.'

Could I really have announced to him that henceforward I forbade him to use my name? I was legally entitled to do so. And this would have given rise to a typically Parisian lawsuit which would have covered me with ridicule.

The character would have acquired a different name. But he would still have been myself, or rather that simplified myself who, according to the author, was going to grow progressively more complex.

The worst of it was that the rascal was quite right and that every month, for years, I was going to find, in a book with a photograph on its cover, a Maigret who imitated me more and more.

And if it had only been in books! The cinema was shortly to take it up, and the radio, and later television.

It's a strange sensation to watch on the screen, coming and going, speaking and blowing his nose, a fellow who pretends to be yourself, who borrows certain of your habits, utters sentences that you have uttered, in circumstances that you have known, through which you have lived, in settings which have sometimes been reconstructed with meticulous care.

Actually the first screen Maigret, Pierre Renoir, was tolerably true to life. I had become a little taller, a little slimmer. The face was different, of course, but certain attitudes were so striking that I suspect the actor of having observed me unawares.

A few months later I grew some six inches shorter, and what I lost in height I gained in stoutness, becoming, in the shape of Abel Tarride, obese and bland, so flabby that I looked like an inflated rubber animal about to float up to the ceiling. Not to mention the knowing winks with which I underlined my own discoveries and my cunning tricks !

I couldn't sit the film out, and my tribulations were not yet over.

Harry Baur was no doubt a great actor, but he was a full twenty years older than myself then, with a cast of features that was flabby and tragic at the same time.

Let's pass over that !

After growing twenty years older, I suddenly grew almost that much younger again, a good deal later, with a certain Préjean, about whom I have no complaint to make – any more than about the rest of them – but who looks far more like certain young detectives of the present generation than those of my own.

And finally, quite lately, I have been made to grow

stout again, almost to bursting point, while I have begun, in the shape of Charles Laughton, to use English as my native tongue.

Well! of all those, there was one at least who had the good taste to cheat Simenon and to consider my truth more valid than his.

It was Pierre Renoir, who did not clap a bowler hat on to his head but wore a perfectly ordinary felt hat, and the sort of clothes worn by any civil servant, whether or not attached to the Police.

I see that I have spoken only of trivial details, a hat, an overcoat, a stove, probably because those details were what first shocked me.

You don't feel any surprise at growing up first, then at growing old. But let a man so much as cut off the tips of his moustaches and he won't recognise himself.

The truth is that I'd like to have finished with what I consider as trivial defects before confronting the two characters on essential points.

If Simenon is right, which is quite possible, my own character will appear odd and involved by the side of that famous simplified – or dressed-up – truth of his, and I shall look like some peevish fellow trying to touch up his own portrait.

Now that I've made a beginning, with the subject of dress, I shall have to go on, if only for my own peace of mind.

Simenon asked me the other day – actually, he has changed too, from the young fellow I met in Xavier

Guichard's office – Simenon asked me, with a touch of mockery:

'Well, what about the new Maigret?'

I tried to answer him in his former words.

'He's taking shape! He's still nothing but a silhouette. A hat, an overcoat. But it's his real hat. His real overcoat! Little by little, perhaps the rest will come, perhaps he'll have arms and legs and even a face, who knows? Perhaps he'll even begin to think by himself, without the aid of a novelist.'

Actually, Simenon is now just about the age I was when we met for the first time. In those days he tended to think of me as a middle-aged man and even, in his heart of hearts, as an elderly one.

I did not ask him what he thought about that today, but I couldn't help remarking:

'D'you know that with the course of time you've begun to walk and smoke your pipe and even to speak like *your* Maigret?'

Which is quite true and which, you'll agree, provided me with a rather piquant revenge.

It was rather as if, after all these years, he had begun to take *himself* for *me*!

# CHAPTER THREE

*In which I shall try to talk about a certain bearded doctor who had some influence on the life of my family and perhaps, all things considered, on my choice of a career.*

I DON'T know if I am going to be able to hit the right tone this time, for I've already filled my wastepaper basket this morning with the pages I've torn up one after the other.

And last night I almost gave the whole thing up.

While my wife was reading what I had written during the day, I watched her, pretending to read my paper as usual, and at a certain point I had the impression that she was surprised, and from then on to the end she kept glancing up at me in astonishment and almost in distress.

Instead of speaking to me immediately, she went to put the manuscript back in the drawer in silence, and it was some time before she said, trying to keep her remark as light as possible :

'Anyone would think you didn't like him.'

I did not need to ask of whom she was speaking, and it was my turn to be perplexed, to stare at her in wide-eyed surprise.

'What are you talking about?' I exclaimed. 'Since when has Simenon ceased to be a friend of ours?'

'Yes, of course . . .'

I wondered what could be at the back of her mind, and tried to recollect what I had written.

'I may be mistaken,' she added. 'Of course I must be mistaken, since you say so. But I had the impression, while reading certain passages, that you felt really resentful about something, and were having your revenge. I don't mean a big, open resentment. Something more secretive, more...'

She did not add the word – but I did so for her – '... more shameful...'

Now Heaven knows how far that was from my mind while I wrote. Not only have I always been on the most cordial terms with Simenon, but he quickly became a family friend of ours, and on the few occasions when we have travelled in the summer holidays it has almost always been to visit him in his various homes, while he was still living in France: in Alsace, at Porquerolles, in the Charente, the Vendée and so forth. More recently, when I agreed to go on a semi-official tour of the U.S.A. it was mainly because I knew I should meet him in Arizona, where he was then living.

'I give you my word...' I began gravely.

'I believe you. But perhaps your readers won't.'

It's my own fault, I'm convinced of it. I am not accustomed to using irony and I realise that I'm probably heavy-handed about it. Whereas on the contrary I had tried, out of diffidence, to treat this difficult subject with a light touch, since it caused me a certain personal embarrassment.

What I am trying to do, in short, is nothing more or less than to size up one image against another image, one character against its double, rather than against its shadow. And Simenon was the first to encourage me in this undertaking.

I add, to pacify my wife, who is fiercely loyal in her friendships, that Simenon, as I said yesterday in other terms, jokingly, is quite different now from the young man whose aggressive self-confidence occasionally made me wince; that on the contrary he himself is inclined to be taciturn nowadays, and speaks with a certain hesitancy, particularly about any subject on which he feels strongly, reluctant to make assertions and, I'd take my oath, seeking my approval.

Having said that much, am I to go on teasing him? Just a little, after all. This'll be the last time, no doubt. It's too good an opportunity, and I cannot resist it.

In the forty-odd volumes he has devoted to my investigations, there are perhaps a score of allusions to my origins, to my family, a few words about my father and his profession as estate-manager, one mention of the Collège de Nantes where I was partly educated, and other brief allusions to my two years as medical student.

And this was the same man who took over four hundred pages to tell the story of his own childhood up to the age of sixteen. It makes no difference that he did so in fictional form, and that his characters may or may not have been true to life, the fact remains that he did not consider his hero complete without the company of his parents and grandparents, his uncles and aunts, whom he describes with all their failings and complaints, their petty vices and their ulcers, while even the neighbour's dog is allotted half a page.

I am not objecting to this, and if I comment on it, it's an indirect way of forestalling any accusation that could be levelled at me of being too longwinded about my own family.

To my mind, a man without a past isn't a whole man. In the course of certain investigations, I have sometimes spent more time over the family and background of a suspect than over the suspect himself, and this has often provided the key to what might otherwise have remained a mystery.

It has been said, quite correctly, that I was born in Central France, not far from Moulins, but I don't think it has ever been specified that the estate of which my father was manager was one of seven and a half thousand acres and included no less than twenty-six small farms.

Not only was my grandfather, whom I remember, one of these tenant farmers, but he followed at least three generations of Maigrets who had tilled the same soil.

An epidemic of typhus, while my father was still young, had decimated his family, which included seven or eight children, and left only two survivors, my father and a sister who was later to marry a baker and settle at Nantes.

Why did my father go to the lycée at Moulins, thus breaking with such old traditions? I have reason to believe that the village priest took an interest in him. But it did not mean a break with the land, for after two years at an agricultural school he came back to the village and joined the staff at the château as assistant estate manager.

I always feel a certain embarrassment when speaking about him. I have the impression, indeed, that people think:

'He has retained a child's picture of his parents.'

And for a long time I wondered whether possibly I was mistaken, whether my critical sense were not failing me.

But I have had occasion to meet other men of the same type, particularly among those of his generation, mostly from the same social class, which might be described as an intermediary one.

For my grandfather, the family at the château, their rights, their privileges, their behaviour were not subjects for discussion. What he thought of them in his heart of hearts I never discovered. I was quite a youngster when he died. I'm convinced none the less, when I remember certain looks of his, certain silences particularly, that his approval was not always passive, was not even always approval, nor yet resignation, but that it proceeded, on the contrary, from a certain pride and above all from a highly developed sense of duty.

This was the feeling that persisted in men like my father, mingled with a reserve, a sense of propriety which may have looked like resignation.

I can picture him very well. I have kept some photographs of him. He was very tall, very thin, his thinness emphasised by narrow trousers, bound in by leather gaiters to just below the knee. I always saw my father in leather gaiters. They were a sort of uniform for him. He wore no beard, but a long sandy moustache in which, when he came home in winter, I used to feel tiny ice-crystals when I kissed him.

Our house stood in the courtyard of the château, a pretty house of rose-coloured brick, one storey high, over-looking the low buildings in which lived several families of farm-hands, grooms and gamekeepers, whose wives for the most part worked at the château as laundresses, needle women or kitchen helps.

Within that courtyard my father was a kind of ruler to whom men spoke respectfully, cap in hand.

About once a week he used to drive off at nightfall, sometimes at dusk, with one or more farmers, to go and buy or sell livestock at some distant fair from which he only returned at the end of the following day.

His office was in a separate building, and on its walls hung photographs of prize oxen or horses, calendars of fairs and, almost invariably, the finest sheaf of wheat harvested on the estate, shrivelling up as the months went by.

About ten o'clock he used to cross the courtyard and go into a private part of the grounds. He would walk round the buildings until he came to the big flight of steps up which the peasants never went, and remained closeted for a time behind the thick walls of the château.

It was for him, in a word, what our morning con-ferences are for us at Headquarters, and as a child I felt proud to see him, very upright, without a trace of servility, as he climbed that awe-inspiring flight of steps.

He spoke little, and he seldom laughed, but when this did happen it was a surprise to discover how young, almost childish, his laugh was, and to see how much simple pleasantries amused him.

He never drank, unlike most of the people I knew. At each meal a small decanter was set aside for him, half filled with a light white wine harvested on the estate, and I never saw him drink anything else, even at weddings or funerals. And at fairs, where he was obliged to stay at inns, he had a cup of his favourite coffee sent up from the kitchen.

I thought of him as a grown man, and even as a middle-aged one. I was five when my grandfather died. As for my mother's parents, they lived over fifty miles away, and we only visited them twice a year, so that I never knew them well. They were not farming folk. They kept a grocer's shop in a largish village, with a café attached to it, as is often the case in country places.

I am not sure, in retrospect, that this was not the reason why our relations with our in-laws were not closer.

I was not quite eight years old when I finally realised that my mother was pregnant. By remarks overheard by chance, by whispers, I more or less grasped that the thing was unexpected, that after my birth the doctors had declared that she was unlikely to have any more children.

I reconstructed all this later, bit by bit, and I suppose this is always the case with childhood memories.

There was at this time in the neighbouring village, which was bigger than ours, a doctor with a pointed red beard whose name was Gadelle – Victor Gadelle if I am not mistaken – about whom people talked a great deal, almost always with an air of mystery, and, probably on account of his beard, and also on account of all that was said about him, I was almost inclined to take him for a kind of devil.

There was a drama in his life, a real drama, the first I ever came across and one which impressed me deeply, particularly as it was to have a profound influence on our family, and thereby on my whole existence.

Gadelle drank. He drank more heavily than any peasant in the neighbourhood, not only from time to time but every day, beginning in the morning and only stopping at night. He drank so much that, in a warm room, the atmosphere would be pervaded by a smell of alcohol which I always sniffed with disgust.

Moreover he was careless of his person. In fact you might have called him dirty.

How, under these conditions, could he have been my father's friend? That remained a mystery to me. The fact remains that he often came to see him and chat with him at our home and that there was even a ritual, which consisted of taking out of the glass-fronted sideboard, as soon as he arrived, a small decanter of brandy that was kept for his exclusive use.

About the original drama I knew almost nothing at the time. Doctor Gadelle's wife was pregnant, and this must have been for the sixth or seventh time. I thought of her as

53

an old woman already, whereas she was probably about forty.

What had happened on the day of her confinement? Apparently Gadelle came home more drunk than usual, and, while waiting for his wife's delivery, went on drinking at her bedside.

As it happened, the first stages of her labour were unusually prolonged. The children had been taken to some neighbour's. Towards morning, as nothing seemed to be happening, the sister-in-law who had spent the night at the house went off to see to things at her own home.

Then, apparently, a great noise was heard in the doctor's house, with cries, and footsteps coming and going.

When people got there, they found Gadelle weeping in a corner. His wife was dead. So was the child.

And for a long time after I would overhear the village gossips whispering in each other's ears, with expressions of indignation or horror :

'A real shambles !'

.        .        .

For months the case of Doctor Gadelle was the main topic of conversation, and, as was to be expected, the neighbourhood was split into two factions.

Some people – and there was a good number of them – went into town, which was quite a journey in those days, to consult a different doctor, while others, through indifference or because they still trusted him, went on sending for the bearded doctor.

My father never took me into his confidence on this subject. I am therefore reduced to conjecture.

Gadelle, at any rate, never stopped coming to see us. He called on us as he had always done, in the course of his rounds, and the familiar gilt-edged decanter was put before him as usual.

He was drinking less, however. People said they never saw him tipsy now. One night he was sent for to the remotest of the farms for a confinement, and he acquitted himself with honour. On his way home he called at our house, and I remember he was very pale; I can still see my father clasping his hand with unwonted persistence as though to encourage him, as though to tell him : 'You see, things weren't so hopeless after all.'

For my father never gave up hope of people. I never heard him utter an irrevocable judgment, even when the black sheep of the estate, a foul-mouthed farmer of whose malpractices he had had to complain to the landlord, had accused him of some dishonest trick or other.

It's quite certain that if, after the death of Gadelle's wife and child, there had been nobody to stretch out a helping hand to the doctor, he would have been a lost man.

My father did so. And when my mother was pregnant, a certain feeling which I find it hard to explain, but which I understand, obliged him to see the thing through.

He took precautions, none the less. Twice, during the last stage of her pregnancy, he took my mother into Moulins to consult a specialist.

When her time came, a stable lad went on horseback to fetch the doctor in the middle of the night. I wasn't sent away from home, but stayed there shut up in my own room, in a great state of agitation, although like all country lads I had acquired a certain knowledge of these things at an early age.

My mother died at seven in the morning, as day was breaking, and when I went downstairs the first thing that caught my eye, in spite of my emotion, was the decanter on the dining-room table.

I was left an only child. A local girl was brought in to look after the house and take care of me. I never saw Doctor Gadelle cross our threshold since that day, but neither did I ever hear my father say one word about him.

A blurred and colourless period followed this drama. I went to the village school. My father spoke less and less. He was thirty-two, and only now do I realise how young he was.

I did not protest when, on completing my twelfth year, I was sent as a boarder to the lycée at Moulins, since it was impossible to take me there every day.

I only stayed there a few months. I was unhappy there, an utter stranger in a new world that felt hostile to me. I said nothing about it to my father, who fetched me home every Saturday evening. I never complained.

He must have understood, for during the Easter holidays his sister, whose husband had opened a bakery at Nantes, suddenly came to see us, and I realised that they were discussing a plan already sketched out by letter.

My aunt, who had a very high colour, had begun to put on weight. She was childless and this grieved her.

For several days she hovered round me anxiously, telling me about the house at Nantes with its good smell of new bread.

She seemed very cheerful. I had guessed. I was resigned. Or, more precisely, since that's a word I don't care for, I had accepted.

My father and I had a long talk together as we walked through the countryside one Sunday morning after Mass. It was the first time he had talked to me as if I were a man. He was considering my future, the impossibility of studying if I stayed in the village, and if I remained at Moulins as a boarder the absence of normal family life.

I know now what he was thinking. He had realised that the company of a man like himself, who had withdrawn into himself and lived mainly with his own thoughts, was not desirable for a young boy who still had everything to hope for from life.

I went off with my aunt, a big trunk jolting behind us, in the cart that took us to the station.

My father did not shed a tear. Neither did I.

.        .        .

That's more or less all I know about him. For years, at Nantes, I was the nephew of the baker and the baker's wife, and I almost got used to the man whom I saw every day with his shaggy chest glowing in the red light of his oven.

I used to spend all my holidays with my father. I won't

go so far as to say we were strangers to one another. But I had my own private life, my ambitions, my problems.

He was my father, whom I loved and respected, but whom I'd given up trying to understand. And it went on like that for years. Is this always the case? I'm inclined to think so.

When my curiosity reawakened, it was too late to ask the questions which I so longed to ask then, and which I reproached myself for not asking when he was still there to answer me.

My father had died of pleurisy at the age of forty-four.

I was a young man, I had begun my medical studies. On my last visits to the château I had been struck by the flush on my father's cheekbones and the hectic glitter of his eyes at night.

'Has there ever been any tuberculosis in our family?' I asked my aunt one day.

She said, as though I had spoken of some shameful taint :

'Good heavens, no! All of them were as tough as oaktrees! Don't you remember your grandfather?'

I did remember him, precisely. I remembered a certain dry cough which he put down to smoking. And as far back as I could remember I always pictured my father with the same cheekbones under which a fire seemed to be glowing.

My aunt had the same pink flush too.

'It's from always living in the heat of a bakery,' she would retort.

She died, none the less, from the same illness as her brother, ten years later.

As for myself, when I got back to Nantes to collect my belongings before starting on a new life, I hesitated for a long while before calling on one of my professors at his private house and asking him to examine me.

'No danger of anything like that,' he reassured me.

Two days later I took the train to Paris.

.        .        .

My wife will forgive me this time if I hark back to Simenon and his picture of me, for I want to discuss a point raised by him in one of his latest books, which concerns me very closely.

It is indeed one of the points that vexed me most – and I'm not referring to such petty questions as dress, which I raised as a joke.

I should not be my father's son if I were not somewhat touchy about all that concerns my job, my career, and that's precisely the question.

I have sometimes had an uneasy feeling that Simenon was somehow trying to apologise for me to the public for entering the police force. And I am sure that in some people's eyes I only took up this profession as a last resort.

Now it is certainly a fact that I had begun my medical studies and that I chose that profession of my own free will, without being pushed into it by somewhat ambitious parents, as often happens.

I had not thought about the matter for years, and it had never occurred to me to ask myself any questions about it, when, precisely on account of something that had been written about my vocation, the problem gradually forced itself upon me.

I spoke to nobody about it, not even to my wife. Today I have to overcome certain feelings of diffidence to put things in their true light, or try to do so.

In one of his books, then, Simenon has spoken of 'a man who mends destinies', and he did not invent the phrase, which was one of my own, which I must have uttered one day when we were chatting together.

Now I wonder if it didn't all spring from Gadelle, whose tragic story, as I subsequently realised, must have struck me far more than I supposed.

Because he was a doctor, because he had failed, the medical profession had acquired in my eyes an extraordinary prestige, it seemed almost a sort of priesthood.

For years, without realising it, I tried to understand the drama of this man at grips with a destiny that was too great for him.

And I remembered my father's attitude towards him, I wondered whether my father had understood the same thing that I had, whether that was why, at whatever cost to himself, he had let the man try his luck.

From Gadelle I went on instinctively to consider the majority of the people I had known, almost all of them simple folk with apparently straightforward lives, who none the less had had at one time or another to measure themselves against destiny.

Don't forget that I am trying to set down here not the reflections of a mature man but the workings of a boy's mind, then of a youth's.

My mother's death seemed to me so stupid a drama, so unnecessary.

And all the other dramas that I knew, all these failures plunged me into a sort of furious despair.

Could nobody do anything about them? Might there not be, somewhere, some man wiser or more experienced than the rest – whom I pictured more or less in the shape of a family doctor, of a Gadelle who was not a failure – capable of telling them gently, firmly :

'You're taking a wrong turn. By acting thus you're heading for disaster. Your right place is here rather than there.'

I think that was it; I felt dimly that too many people were not in their right places, that they were striving to play parts that were beyond their capacities, so that the game was lost for them before they started.

Above all, please don't imagine that I ever dreamed of becoming that sort of God-the-Father-figure myself.

After trying to understand Gadelle, and then to understand my father's attitude towards him, I went on looking around me asking the same questions.

One example may raise a smile. There were fifty-eight of us in my class one year, fifty-eight pupils with different social backgrounds, different qualities, ambitions and failings. Now I had amused myself working out the ideal destiny of all my fellow-pupils and, in my mind, I called them : 'the lawyer . . . the tax-collector . . .'

For quite a while, too, I exercised my wits in guessing what the people I came across would eventually die of.

Is it clearer now why I wanted to become a doctor? The word police, for me, suggested at that time merely the constable at the street corner, And if I had heard speak of the secret police, I had not the least conception what it could be.

And then suddenly I had to earn my living. I arrived in Paris without even the vaguest notion of what career I was to choose. In view of my unfinished studies I could at best hope for some office job, and it was with this in mind that, without enthusiasm, I started reading the 'small ads' in the newspapers. My uncle had in vain offered to teach me his trade and keep me at the bakery.

In the little hotel where I was staying, on the Left Bank, there lived on the same landing as myself a man who aroused my curiosity, a man of about forty who, Heaven knows why, reminded me somewhat of my father.

Physically, indeed, he was as different as possible from the fair, lean, slope-shouldered man whom I had always seen wearing leather gaiters. He was rather short and squat, dark-haired, with a prematurely bald patch which he concealed by carefully combing his hair forward, and black moustaches with curled tips.

He was always neatly dressed in black, wore an over-coat with a velvet collar, which accounts for a certain other overcoat, and carried a stick with a solid silver knob.

I think the likeness to my father lay in his bearing, in a certain way of walking without ever hurrying, of listening, of watching, and then, somehow, of withdrawing within himself.

I met him by chance in a homely restaurant in the neighbourhood; I discovered that he took his evening meal there almost every day and I began, for no definite reason, to want to get to know him.

In vain did I try to guess what his occupation in life might be. He must be unmarried, since he lived alone at the hotel. I used to hear him get up in the morning and come back at night at irregular hours.

He never had any visitors and, the only time I met him with a companion, he was standing at the corner of the Boulevard Saint-Michel talking to an individual of such unprepossessing appearance that one might unhesitatingly have described him, at that period, as an *apache*.

I was on the point of taking a job in a firm that made *passementerie*, in the Rue des Victoires. I was to call there next day with references for which I had written to my former teachers.

That evening at the restaurant, moved by some instinct or other, I decided to rise from table just as my hotel neighbour was replacing his napkin in his pigeonhole, so that I happened to be there to hold the door open for him.

He must have noticed me. Perhaps he had guessed that I wanted to speak to him, for he gave me a long look.

'Thank you,' he said.

Then, as I was standing still on the pavement:

'Are you going back to the hotel?'

'I think so . . . I don't know . . .'

It was a fine late-autumn night. The river bank was not far off, and the moon was visible rising behind the trees.

'Alone in Paris?'

'I'm alone, yes.'

Without asking for my company, he accepted it, he took it for granted as a *fait accompli*.

'You're looking for work?'

'How do you know?'

He did not even trouble to answer and slipped a cachou between his lips. I was soon to understand why. He was afflicted with bad breath and knew it.

'You're from the provinces?'

'From Nantes, but I come from the country originally.'

I spoke freely to him. It was practically the first time since I had come to Paris that I had found a companion, and his silence did not embarrass me at all, no doubt because I was used to my father's friendly silences.

I had told him almost the whole of my story when we reached the Quai des Orfèvres, on the other side of the Pont Saint-Michel.

He stopped in front of a great door that was standing ajar, and said to me:

'Will you wait a moment for me? I shall only be a few minutes.'

A policeman in uniform was on duty at the door. After pacing up and down for a moment I asked him:

'Isn't this the Palais de Justice?'

'This is the entry to Police Headquarters.'

My hotel neighbour was called Jacquemain. He was, in fact, unmarried, as I learned that evening while we were walking up and down the Seine, crossing the same bridges over and over again, with the massive Palais de Justice almost continuously towering over us.

He was a Detective-Inspector and he told me about his profession, as briefly as my father would have done of his, with the same underlying pride.

He was killed three years later, before I had myself acquired access to those offices in the Quai des Orfèvres which had come to hold such glamour for me. It happened in the neighbourhood of the Porte d'Italie, during a street fight. A bullet which was not even intended for him hit him right in the chest.

His photograph still hangs among the rest in one of those black frames surmounted by the inscription: 'Died in the performance of his duty.'

He didn't talk to me much. He chiefly listened to me. This did not restrain me from asking him, towards eleven o'clock that night, in a voice quivering with impatience:

'Do you really think it's possible?'

'I'll give you an answer tomorrow evening.'

Of course there was no question of my going straight into the Sûreté. The age of diplomas had not yet arrived, and everyone had to start in the ranks. My only ambition was to be accepted, in any capacity, in one of the Paris police stations, and to be allowed to discover for myself an aspect of the world of which Inspector Jacquemain had merely given me a glimpse.

Just as we were parting on the landing of our hotel, which has since been pulled down, he asked :

'Would you very much dislike wearing uniform?'

I felt a slight shock, I must admit, a brief hesitation which did not escape his notice and which can scarcely have pleased him.

'No . . .' I replied in a low voice.

And I wore it, not for long, for seven or eight months. As I had long legs and was very lean, very swift, strange as that may seem today, they gave me a bicycle and, in order that I might get to know Paris, where I was always losing my way, I was given the job of delivering notes to the various police stations.

Has Simenon talked about all this? I don't remember. For months, perched on my bicycle, I threaded my way between cabs and double-decker buses, still horse-drawn, of which I was horribly frightened, particularly when they were tearing down from Montmartre.

Officials still wore frock-coats and top-hats and, above a certain rank, they sported morning-coats.

Policemen were mostly middle-aged men with reddish noses who were to be seen drinking at bar-counters with coachmen and of whom song-writers made relentless fun.

I was unmarried. I felt shy of going courting in uniform, and I decided that my real life would only begin on the day when I should enter the house in the Quai des

Orfèvres as a detective, using the main staircase, and not merely as a messenger carrying official notes.

When I mentioned this ambition to my hotel neighbour, he did not smile, but looked at me reflectively and murmured :

'Why not?'

I did not know that I was so soon to attend his funeral. My forecasts about human destiny were still not entirely adequate.

# CHAPTER FOUR

*How I ate* petits fours *at Anselme and Geraldine's,*
*thereby shocking the Highways and Bridges*

DID my father or my grandfather ever wonder whether
they might have become something other than what they
were? Had they ever had other ambitions? Did they envy
a different lot from their own?

It's strange to have lived with people for so long and
yet to know nothing of what nowadays would seem essential. I have often asked myself the question, with the
feeling that I was straddling two worlds, totally foreign
to one another.

We talked about it not long ago, Simenon and I, in my
flat in the Boulevard Richard-Lenoir. I think it may have
been on the eve of his departure for the United States. He
had paused to stare at the enlarged photograph of my
father, although he had seen it for years hanging on the
dining-room wall.

While he studied it with particular attention, he kept
casting searching glances at me, as if he were trying to
make comparisons, and this set him pondering.

'The fact is,' he finally remarked, 'you were born in an
ideal milieu, Maigret, at the ideal moment in a family's
evolution, to become a top-rank official.'

I was struck by this comment, because I had already
thought about it, in a less precise and above all a less

personal fashion; I had noticed how many of my colleagues came from peasant families having quite recently
lost direct contact with the land.

Simenon went on, almost regretfully and as though he
envied me:

'I'm a whole generation ahead of you. I have to go
back to my grandfather to find the equivalent of your
father. My own father had already reached the civil
servant stage.'

My wife was gazing at him attentively, trying to understand, and he added in a lighter tone:

'In the normal course of events I'd have had to make
my way up from the bottom in some profession, and work
hard to become a G.P. or a lawyer or an engineer. Or
else...'

'Or else what?'

'To become an embittered rebel. Of course that's what
usually happens. Otherwise there'd be a plethora of
doctors and lawyers. I think I come from the stock that
has provided the greatest number of misfits.'

I don't know why this conversation has suddenly re-
curred to me. Probably because I'm recollecting my early
years and trying to analyse my frame of mind at that
period.

I was all alone in the world. I had just landed in an
unfamiliar city in which wealth was flaunted more
blatantly than today.

Two things struck one: that wealth on the one hand,

and that poverty on the other; and I belonged to the second group.

A whole social set, in full view of the masses, lived a life of sophisticated leisure, and the newspapers reported all the doings of these people who had no other preoccupation than their own pleasures and vanities.

Now not for one moment did I feel tempted to rebel. I did not envy them. I did not hope to be like them one day. I did not contrast my lot with theirs.

For me they belonged to a world as different from mine as if it had been another planet.

I remember that in those days I had an insatiable appetite, which had already been legendary when I was a child. At Nantes my aunt used often to tell how she had seen me eat a four-pound loaf when I got back from school, which did not prevent me from having dinner a couple of hours later.

I earned very little money, and my great concern was to satisfy that hunger of mine; I looked for luxury not on the terraces of the famous boulevard cafés, nor in the shop-windows of the Rue de la Paix, but more prosaically on pork-butchers' counters.

In the streets through which I usually passed I had discovered a number of pork-butchers' shops, which fascinated me, and in the days when I still travelled about Paris in uniform, perched on a bicycle, I used to calculate my time so as to save the few minutes necessary to buy a piece of sausage or a slice of pâté, and devour it, with a roll from the nearby bakery, while standing on the pavement outside.

When my stomach was appeased I felt happy and full of self-confidence. I did my job conscientiously. I attached importance to the slightest tasks entrusted to me. And there was no question of overtime. I considered that all of my time belonged to the police, and it seemed to be quite natural that I should be kept at work for fourteen or fifteen hours at a stretch.

If I mention this it is not that I want to take any credit for it, but rather, on the contrary, because as far as I can remember it was a common attitude at that time.

Very few police constables had more than a primary education. On account of Inspector Jacquemain, the authorities knew – although I myself didn't then know who knew, or even that anyone knew – that I had begun advanced studies. After a few months I was greatly surprised to find myself appointed to a post which I had never dared to hope for : that of Secretary to the Station Officer of the Saint-Georges district.

And yet the job had an unglamorous name at the time. It was called 'being the Station Officer's dog'.

My bicycle, my cap and my uniform were taken away from me. So was my chance of stopping at pork butchers' on my way through the Paris streets.

I was particularly grateful for the fact of being in plain clothes when one day, walking along the pavement of the Boulevard Saint-Michel, I heard a voice hailing me.

A tall fellow in a white overall was running after me.

'Jubert!' I cried.

'Maigret!'

'What are you doing here?'

'And you?'

'Listen. I daren't stop out just now. Come and pick me up at seven o'clock at the door of the chemist's shop.'

Jubert, Felix Jubert, was one of my fellow students from the medical school at Nantes. I knew he had broken off his studies at the same time as myself, but, I believe, for different reasons. Without actually being a dunce, he was slow-witted, and I remember they used to say about him:

'He works so hard he comes out in spots, but he's no wiser next day.'

He was very tall and bony, with a big nose, coarse features, red hair, and as long as I'd known him his face had always been covered, not with those small acne pimples that are the bane of young men's lives, but with big red or purple spots which he spent hours smothering in medicated ointments and powders.

I went along to wait for him that same evening at the chemist's shop where he had been working for some weeks. He had no relatives in Paris. He was living in the Cherche-Midi district with people who took in two or three lodgers.

'And what are you doing yourself?'

'I'm in the police force.'

I can still picture his violet eyes, clear as a girl's, trying to conceal their incredulity. His voice sounded quite odd as he repeated :

'The police force?'

He was staring at my suit, instinctively looking for the constable on duty at the corner of the boulevard as though to make a comparison.

'I'm secretary to the Station Officer.'

'Oh, good, I understand.'

Whether from conventional pride, or, more likely, because of my own inability to explain myself and his inability to understand, I did not confess that three weeks earlier I had still been wearing uniform, and that my ambition was to join the detective force.

In his opinion and in that of a great many people, a secretary's was a good, respectable job; I sat at a desk, nice and clean, with books in front of me and a pen in my hand.

'Have you many friends in Paris?'

Apart from Inspector Jacquemain I really knew nobody, for at the police station I was still a novice and people had to watch me before they would make friends with me.

'No girl friend either? What do you do with all your spare time?'

In the first place I hadn't much of that. And in the second, I spent it studying, for in order to reach my aim faster I had resolved to pass the examinations which had just been instituted.

We dined together that evening. Towards the end of the meal he told me, as if promising me a treat :

'I shall have to introduce you.'

'To whom?'

'To some very nice people. Friends of mine. You'll see.'

He gave no further explanation that first day. And I don't know why, it was several weeks before we saw each other again. I might quite well never have seen him again. I had not given him my address. I had not got his. It never occurred to me to go and wait for him outside the chemist's shop.

Chance, once again, brought us face to face at the door of the Théâtre Fıançais, where we were both queuing.

'Isn't it silly,' he said. 'I thought I'd lost you. I don't even know at which police station you're working. I mentioned you to my friends.'

He had a way of talking about these friends which suggested that they were a very special set of people, almost a mysterious sect.

'You've got a dress suit, I hope?'

'I've got one.'

It was pointless to add that it had been my father's dress suit, which was somewhat old-fashioned, since he had worn it at his wedding, and which I'd had cut to fit me.

'I'll take you there on Friday. You must manage to be free without fail on Friday evening at eight o'clock. Can you dance?'

'No.'

'It doesn't matter. But it would be better if you took a few lessons. I know a good school that's not expensive. I've been to it myself.'

This time he had made a note of my address and even of the little restaurant where I used to have dinner when I was not on duty, and on Friday evening he was in my room, sitting on my bed, while I dressed.

'I must explain to you, so that you don't drop any bricks. We shall be the only people there, you and I, who aren't connected with the Highways and Bridges Department. A distant cousin of mine, whom I happened to run into, introduced me. Monsieur and Madame Léonard are charming people. Their niece is the loveliest girl in the world.'

I gathered at once that he was in love with her and that it was in order to show me the object of his passion that he was dragging me off with him.

'There'll be others, you needn't worry,' he promised me. 'Very nice girls.'

As it was raining and we didn't want to arrive covered with mud, we took a cab, the first cab I had ever taken in Paris except on duty. I can still picture our white shirt-fronts as we passed under the gas lamps. And I can picture Felix Jubert stopping the cab in front of a florist's shop so that we might decorate our buttonholes.

'Old Monsieur Léonard,' he explained, 'Anselme they call him, retired about ten years ago. Before that he was one of the top officials in the Highways and Bridges Department, and even now his successors still come to consult

him sometimes. His niece's father is in Highways and
Bridges too, on the administrative side. And so is all their
family, so to speak.'

To hear him talk of this government service you realised
that for Jubert it was Paradise Lost, that he would have
given anything not to have wasted those precious years
studying medicine, so that he too could have made a start
on such a career.

'You'll see!'

And I saw. It was in the Boulevard Beaumarchais, not
far from the Place de la Bastille, in an oldish but comfortable and fairly well-to-do block. All the windows were lit
up on the third floor, and Jubert's upward glance as we
got out of the cab showed me clearly that the party in
question was being held there.

I felt rather ill at ease. I began to wish I hadn't come.
My stiff collar hurt me; I was convinced that my tie was
getting twisted and that one of the tails of my coat tended
to curl up like a cock's crest.

The stair was dimly lit, the steps covered with a crimson
carpet that seemed to me sumptuous. And the landing
windows were filled with stained glass which for a long
time I considered the last word in refinement.

Jubert had smeared his spotty face with a thicker coat
of ointment, which for some reason gave it a purplish
sheen. He reverently pulled a big tassel which hung in
front of a door. Within, we could hear the buzz of conversation, with that touch of shrillness in voices and

laughter which suggests the excitement of a social gathering.

A maid in a white apron opened the door to us, and Felix, as he held out his overcoat, was delighted to show himself a regular frequenter of the house by remarking:

'Good evening, Clémence.'

'Good evening, Monsieur Felix.'

The drawing-room was fairly big, rather dimly lighted, with a great deal of dark upholstery, and in the next room, visible through a wide glass partition, the furniture had been pushed against the wall so as to leave the floor free for dancing.

With a protective air Jubert led me up to an old white-haired lady sitting by the fireside.

'May I introduce my friend Maigret, about whom I had the honour of telling you, and who was most anxious to pay you his respects in person.'

No doubt he had been rehearsing his sentence all the way there, and was watching to see if I was making a proper bow, did not seem too ill at ease, and in short was doing him credit.

The old lady was charming, tiny, with delicate features and a lively expression, but I was disconcerted when she said to me with a smile:

'Why don't you belong to the Highways and Bridges? I'm sure Anselme will be sorry.'

Her name was Géraldine. Anselme, her husband, was sitting in another armchair, so still that you'd have thought he had been carried in bodily and set down there to be displayed like a waxwork figure. He was very old. I learned later that he was well over eighty and Géraldine just that age.

Somebody was playing the piano softly, a podgy youth in a tight coat, while a girl in a pale blue dress turned the pages for him. I could only see her from the back. When I was introduced to her I dared not look her in the face, so embarrassed did I feel at being there, not knowing what to say or where to stand.

Dancing had not yet begun. On a small table there stood a tray of *petits fours*, and a little later, as Jubert had left me to my fate, I went up to it, I still don't know why, certainly not out of greed, for I wasn't hungry and I have never liked *petits fours*, probably to keep m,self in countenance.

I took one mechanically. Then a second. Somebody said :

'Hush !'

And a second girl, this time one in a pink dress, with a slight squint, began to sing, standing beside the piano, on which she leaned with one hand, while waving a fan with the other.

I kept on eating. I was not conscious of it. I was still less conscious that the old lady was watching me with stupefaction, then that others, noticing my performance, couldn't take their eyes off me.

One of the young men made some remark to his neighbour and once again somebody said : 'Hush !'

You could count the girls by the light-coloured patches

they made against the men's black coats. There were four of them. Jubert apparently was trying to attract my attention without success, in great distress at seeing me pick up *petits fours* one by one and eat them conscientiously. He later admitted that he had felt sorry for me, being convinced I had had no dinner.

Others must have thought the same thing. The song ended. The girl in pink bowed, and everybody clapped; and then I noticed that I was the centre of all attention as I stood there beside the little table, my mouth full and a biscuit in my hand.

I was about to disappear without apologies, to beat a retreat, to run away, literally, from the room and the lively crowd that was so utterly foreign to me.

Just then, in a shadowy corner, I caught sight of a face, the face of the girl in blue, and on that face a gentle, reassuring, almost friendly expression. It looked as if she had understood me and was encouraging me.

The maid came in with refreshments, and after having eaten so much at the wrong time I dared not take a glass when it was offered me.

'Louise, won't you pass round the *petits fours*?'

That was how I learned that the girl in blue was called Louise and that she was the niece of M. and Mme Léonard.

She waited on everybody before coming up to me, and then, pointing to some cake or other on which there was a small preserved fruit, she said to me with an air of complicity :

79

'They've left the nicest. Just taste those.'

The only answer I could find was :

'Really ?'

Those were the first words that passed between Madame Maigret and myself.

. . .

Presently, when she reads what I've been writing, I know she'll shrug her shoulders, murmuring :

'What's the good of telling all that ?'

Actually, she's delighted with Simenon's picture of her, the picture of a good housewife, always busy cooking and polishing, always fussing over her great baby of a husband. It was even on account of that picture, I suspect, that she was the first to become his staunch friend, to the extent of considering him as one of the family and of defending him when I haven't dreamed of attacking him.

Now this portrait, like all portraits, is far from being strictly accurate. When I met her on that memorable evening she was a rather plump young girl with a very fresh face and a sparkle in her eyes that was lacking in her friends'.

What would have happened if I hadn't eaten those cakes? It's quite possible that she would never have noticed me among the dozen or so young men there who all, except my friend Jubert, belonged to Highways and Bridges.

Those three words, Highways and Bridges, have retained an almost comic significance for us, and if either of us utters them it sets us both smiling; if we hear the words spoken somewhere we cannot, even now, help casting a knowing glance at one another.

To do things properly I ought here to insert the whole genealogy of the Schöllers, Kurts and Léonards, which I found most confusing for a long time, and which represents my wife's side of the family.

If you go anywhere in Alsace between Strasburg and Mulhouse you'll probably hear speak of them. I think it was a Kurt from Scharrachbergheim who first, under Napoleon, founded the almost dynastic tradition of Highways and Bridges. Apparently he was quite famous in his day, and he married into the Schöller family, who were in the same Government service.

The Léonards in their turn entered the family, and since then, from father to son, from brother to brother-in-law or cousin, practically everybody has belonged to the same organisation, to such an extent that it was considered a comedown for a Kurt to become one of the biggest brewers in Colmar.

I only guessed at all this that first evening, thanks to the few hints that Jubert had given me.

And when we went out into the driving rain, not bothering this time to take a cab, which, in any case, we'd have had difficulty in finding in that district, I had almost begun to feel regretfully that I'd chosen the wrong career myself.

'What d'you think of that?'

'Of what?'

'Of what Louise did! I'm not going to scold you. But it was a very awkward situation. Did you see how tactfully she put you at your ease, without showing it? She's an amazing girl. Alice Perret may be more brilliant, but . . .'

I didn't know who Alice Perret was. The only person who had made any impression on me that whole evening was the girl in pale blue, who, between dances, had come to chat with me.

'Alice is the one who sang. I think she's going to get engaged to the boy who came with her, Louis, whose parents are very rich.'

We parted very late that night. At every fresh downpour we went into some bistro that was still open, to take shelter and drink a cup of coffee. Felix would not let me go, talking unceasingly about Louise, trying to make me admit that she was the ideal girl.

'I know I don't stand much chance. It's because her parents want to find her a husband in Highways and Bridges that they've sent her to stay with her uncle Léonard. You see, there are no more available at Colmar or at Mulhouse, or else they're in the family already. She's been here two months now. She's to spend the whole winter in Paris.'

'Does she know?'

'What?'

'That she's supposed to marry into Highways and Bridges.'

'Of course. But she doesn't care. She's a most independent girl, far more so than you might think. You didn't have time to appreciate her. Next Friday you must try and talk to her more. If you could dance, it would make things easier. Why don't you take two or three lessons in the meantime?'

I took no dancing lessons. Which was just as well. For Louise, contrary to the worthy Jubert's belief, disliked nothing so much as gliding round in the arms of a dancing partner.

A fortnight later there occurred a trivial incident which, at the time, seemed of great moment to me – and which perhaps was so, but in a different way.

The young engineers who used to visit the Léonards were an exclusive clique and affected the use of words which had no meaning for anyone outside their own set.

Did I detest them? Most likely. And I objected to their insistent habit of calling me 'the Police Inspector'. It had become a wearisome game.

'Hi, Inspector . . .' they would call to me from one end of the drawing-room to the other.

Now, that particular evening, while Jubert and Louise were chatting in one corner, close to a green plant which I can still picture, a young fellow in glasses went up and whispered something to them, with a laughing glance in my direction.

A few minutes later I asked my friend:

'What was he saying?'

Visibly embarrassed, he said evasively:

'Nothing.'

'Something spiteful?'

'I'll tell you when we're outside.'

The spectacled boy repeated his performance with other groups, and everybody seemed to be having a good laugh at my expense.

Everybody except Louise, who refused a good many dances that evening and spent the time talking to me.

Once outside, I questioned Felix.

'What did he say?'

'Tell me frankly first. What did you do before you became the Station Officer's secretary?'

'Well . . . I was in the police . . .'

'In uniform?'

So that was the great sensation. The spectacled fellow must have recognised me from having seen me in my policeman's outfit.

Just imagine a policeman among the gentlemen from Highways and Bridges!

'What did she say?' I asked, with a lump in my throat.

'She was wonderful. She's always wonderful. You won't believe me, but you'll see . . .'

Poor old Jubert!

'She told him that you must certainly have looked better in uniform than he would.'

Nevertheless, I kept away from the Boulevard Beaumarchais the following Friday. I avoided meeting Jubert. A fortnight later, he came himself to hunt me out.

'Well, they were asking after you on Friday.'

'Who was?'

'Madame Léonard. She asked me if you were unwell.'

'I've been very busy.'

I felt sure that if Madame Léonard had spoken of me it was because of her niece . . .

Now then! I don't think there's any point in going into all these details. It's going to be hard enough to make sure that what I've written already doesn't get thrown into the waste paper basket.

For nearly three months Jubert played his part without suspecting anything, and indeed without our making any effort to deceive him. It was he who used to come and fetch me at my hotel and tie my bow-tie for me on the pretext that I didn't know how to dress. It was he, again, who used to tell me when he saw me sitting by myself :

'You ought to pay some attention to Louise. You're not being polite.'

And when we left, it was always he who insisted :

'You're quite wrong to suppose that she's not interested in you. On the contrary, she's very fond of you. She's always asking me about you.'

Towards Christmas, the girl friend with the squint got engaged to the pianist, and they stopped coming to the Boulevard Beaumarchais.

I don't know if Louise's attitude was beginning to discourage the rest, if we were perhaps less discreet than we imagined. The fact remains that there were gradually fewer guests every Friday at Anselme and Géraldine's.

Jubert finally had it out with me in February, in my room. That Friday, he was not wearing evening dress, as I noticed immediately. He had that look of resigned bitterness that the Comédie Française actors wear in certain famous roles.

'I've come to tie your bow-tie, in spite of everything!' he said with a forced smile.

'You're not free tonight?'

'I'm utterly free, on the contrary, free as the air, freer than I've ever been.'

And standing before me with my white tie in his hand, and his eyes boring into mine:

'Louise has told me all.'

I was dumbfounded. For so far she'd told *me* nothing. And I had told her nothing either.

'What are you talking about?'

'About you and her.'

'But...'

'I put the question to her. I went to see her on purpose yesterday.'

'But what question?'

'I asked her if she would marry me.'

'And she said no?'

'She said no, that she was very fond of me, that I should always be her best friend, but that...'

'Did she mention me?'

'Not exactly.'

'Well then?'

'I've understood! I ought to have understood that first evening, when you ate those *petits fours* and she looked at you indulgently. When a woman looks so indulgently at a man who's behaving as you were...'

86

Poor Jubert! We lost sight of him almost immediately, just as we lost sight of all the Highways and Bridges gentlemen, apart from Uncle Léonard.

For years we never knew what had become of him. And I was getting on for fifty when one day, on the Canebière at Marseilles, I went into a chemist's shop to buy some aspirin. I hadn't read the name on the shop front. I heard an exclamation:

'Maigret!'

'Jubert!'

'What's been happening to you? Silly of me to ask, since I've known all about you from the newspapers for a long time. How is Louise?'

Then he told me about his eldest son who, by a nice irony of fate, was preparing for the Highways and Bridges examination.

.      .      .

With Jubert missing from the Boulevard Beaumarchais, the Friday soirées became even more sparsely attended, and often, now, there was nobody to play the piano. On such occasions Louise would play and I would turn over for her, while one or two couples danced in the dining-room, which had now grown too big.

I don't think I asked Louise if she was willing to marry me. Most of the time we talked about my career, about the police, about a detective's job.

I told her how much I should earn when I was at last appointed to Headquarters, adding that this would take at least three years and that until then my salary would scarcely be adequate to set up house with properly.

I told her, too, about the two or three interviews I had had with Xavier Guichard, who was already our Big Chief, who had not forgotten my father and had more or less taken me under his wing.

'I don't know if you like Paris. For, you see, I shall have to spend all my life in Paris.'

'You can live there as quietly as in the provinces, can't you?'

Finally, one Friday, I found no guests there, only Géraldine who came to open the door to me herself, in her black silk dress, and who said to me in a rather solemn voice :

'Come in !'

Louise was not in the drawing-room. There were no trays of cakes and no refreshments. Spring had come, and there was no fire burning in the hearth. I felt I had nothing to cling on to, and I had kept my hat in my hand, ill at ease in my dress suit and patent leather pumps.

'Tell me, young man, what are your intentions?'

That was probably one of the most painful moments in my life. The voice sounded to me hard and accusing. I dared not raise my eyes, and I could see nothing but the edge of a black dress against the flower-patterned carpet, with the tip of a very pointed shoe showing. My ears turned scarlet.

'I swear . . .' I stammered.

'I'm not asking you to swear, I'm asking you if you intend to marry her.'

I looked at her at last and I don't think I have ever seen an old woman's face expressing so much affectionate mischief.

'But of course!'

Apparently – I've been told so often enough since – I jumped up like a jack-in-the-box and repeated, still louder:

'Of course!'

And I almost shouted a third time:

'Why, of course!'

She did not even raise her voice to call:

'Louise!'

And Louise, who was standing behind a half-open door, came in awkwardly, blushing as much as myself.

'What did I tell you?' said her aunt.

'Why?' I broke in. 'Didn't she believe it?'

'I wasn't sure. It was auntie...'

Let's skip the next scene, for I'm sure my wife would censor it.

Old Léonard, for his part, showed much less enthusiasm, I must admit, and he never forgave me for not belonging to Highways and Bridges. He was very old, almost a centenarian, and riveted to his armchair by his infirmities; he would look at me and shake his head, as if something had gone badly wrong with the way of the world.

'You'll have to take leave to visit Colmar. What about the Easter holidays?'

Old Géraldine wrote herself to Louise's parents, a series of letters – to prepare them for the shock, as she said – breaking the news to them.

At Easter I was allowed barely forty-eight hours' leave. I spent most of it in trains, which were less rapid then than today.

I was given a perfectly proper reception, without rapture.

'The best way to find out if both of you are serious is to keep apart from one another for some time. Louise will spend the summer here. In the autumn you can come back to see us.'

'May I write to her?'

'Within reason. Once a week, for instance.'

It seems funny today. It was not at all funny at the time.

I had promised myself, without a trace of secret spite, to choose Jubert as best man. When I went to try and find him at the chemist's in the Boulevard Saint-Michel he had left, and nobody knew what had become of him.

I spent part of the summer hunting for a flat and I found the one in the Boulevard Richard-Lenoir.

'Until we find something better, you understand? When I'm promoted Inspector . . .'

# CHAPTER FIVE

*Dealing somewhat haphazardly with hobnailed socks,*
apaches, *prostitutes, radiators, pavements and*
*railway stations.*

A FEW years ago some of us talked of founding a sort
of club, more likely a monthly dinner, which was to be
called 'The Hobnailed Socks Club'. We got together for
a drink, in any case, at the Brasserie Dauphine. We
argued about who should and who shouldn't be admitted.
And we wondered quite seriously whether the chaps from
the other branch, I mean from the Rue des Saussaies,
should be considered eligible.

Then, as was only to be expected, things got no further.
At that time there were still at least four of us, among the
inspectors in the Detective Force, who were rather proud
of the nickname 'hobnailed socks' formerly given us by
satirical song-writers, and which certain young detectives
fresh from college sometimes used amongst themselves
when referring to those of their seniors who had risen from
the ranks.

In the old days, indeed, it took a good many years to
win one's stripes, and exams were not enough, A sergeant,
before hoping for promotion, had to have worn out his
shoe-soles in practically every branch of the Force.

It is not easy to convey the meaning of this with any
sort of precision to the younger generation.

'Hobnailed shoes' and 'big moustaches' were the terms that sprang naturally to people's lips when they spoke of the police.

And in fact, for years, I wore hobnailed shoes myself. Not from preference. Not, as caricaturists seemed to imply, because we thought such footwear was the height of elegance and comfort, but for more down-to-earth reasons.

Two reasons, to be exact. The first, that our salary barely enabled us to make ends meet. I often hear people talk of the gay, carefree life at the beginning of this century. Young people refer enviously to the prices current at that time, cigars at two sous, dinner with wine and coffee for twenty sous.

What people forget is that at the outset of his career a public servant earned somewhat under a hundred francs a month.

When I was serving in the Public Highways Squad I would cover during my day, which was often a thirteen or fourteen hour day, miles and miles of pavement in all weathers.

So that one of the first problems of our married life was the problem of getting my shoes soled. At the end of each month, when I brought back my pay-packet to my wife, she would divide its contents into a number of small piles.

'For the butcher . . . For rent . . . For gas . . .'

There was hardly anything left to put in the last pile of small silver.

'For your shoes.'

Our dream was always to buy new ones, but for a long time it was only a dream. Often I went for weeks without confessing to her that my soles, between the hobnails, absorbed the gutter water greedily.

If I mention this here it is not out of bitterness but, on the contrary, quite lightheartedly, and I think it is necessary to give an idea of a police officer's life.

There were no such things as taxis, and even if the streets had been crowded with them they'd have been beyond our reach, as were the cabs which we used only in very special circumstances.

In any case, in the Public Highways Squad, our duty was to keep walking along the pavements, mingling with the crowd from morning till night and from night until morning.

Why, when I think of those days, do I chiefly remember the rain? As if it had rained unceasingly for years, as if the seasons had been different then. Of course, it is because the rain added a number of additional ordeals to one's task. Not only did your socks become soaked. The shoulders of your coat gradually turned into cold compresses, your hat became a waterspout, and your hands, thrust into your coat pockets, grew blue with cold.

The roads were less well lighted than they are today. A certain number of them in the outskirts were unpaved. At night the windows showed as yellowish squares against the blackness, for most of the houses were still lighted with oil lamps or even, more wretchedly still, with candles.

And then there were the *apaches*.

All round the fortifications, in those days, their knives would come into play, and not always for gain, for the sake of the rich man's wallet or watch.

What they wanted chiefly was to prove to themselves that they were men, tough guys, and to win the admiration of the little tarts in black pleated skirts and huge chignons who paced the pavements under the gas jets.

We were unarmed. Contrary to the general belief, a policeman in plain clothes has not the right to carry a revolver in his pocket and if, in certain cases, a man takes one, it's against the regulations and entirely on his own responsibility.

Junior officers could not consider themselves entitled to do so. There were a certain number of streets, in the neighbourhood of La Villette, Ménilmontant and the Porte d'Italie, where one ventured reluctantly and sometimes trembled at the sound of one's own footsteps.

For a long time the telephone remained a legendary luxury beyond the scope of our budgets. When I was delayed several hours, there was no question of ringing up my wife to warn her, so that she used to spend lonely evenings in our gas-lit dining-room, listening for noises on the stairway and warming up the same dish four or five times over.

As for the moustaches with which we were caricatured, we really wore them. A man without a moustache looked like a flunkey.

Mine was longish, reddish brown, somewhat darker than my father's, with pointed ends. Later it dwindled to a toothbrush and then disappeared completely.

It is a fact, moreover, that most police inspectors wore huge jet-black moustaches like those in their caricatures. This is because, for some mysterious reason, for quite a long time, the profession attracted chiefly natives of the Massif Central.

There are few streets in Paris along which I have not trudged, watchful-eyed, and I learned to know all the rank and file of the pavements, from beggars, barrel-organ players and flower-girls to cardsharpers and pickpockets, including prostitutes and the drunken old women who spend most of their nights at the police station.

I 'covered' the Halles at night, the Place Maubert, the quays and the reaches beneath the quays.

I covered crowded gatherings too, the biggest job of all, at the Foire du Trône and the Foire de Neuilly, at Longchamps races and patriotic demonstrations, at military parades, visits from foreign royalties, carriage processions, travelling circuses and second-hand markets.

After a few months, a few years at this job one's head is full of a varied array of figures and faces that remain indelibly engraved on one's memory.

I should like to try – and it's not easy – to give a more or less accurate idea of our relations with these people, including those whom we periodically had to take off to the lock-up.

Needless to say, the picturesque aspect soon ceases to

exist for us. Inevitably, we come to scan the streets of Paris with a professional eye, which fastens on certain familiar details or notices some unusual circumstance and draws the necessary conclusion from it.

When I consider this subject, the thing that strikes me most is the bond that is formed between the policeman and the quarry he has to track down. Above all, except in a few exceptional cases, the policeman is entirely devoid of hatred or even of ill-will.

Devoid of pity, too, in the usual sense of the word.

Our relations, so to speak, are strictly professional.

We have seen too much, as you can well imagine, to be shocked any longer by certain forms of wretchedness or depravity. So that the latter does not arouse our indignation, nor does the former cause us that distress felt by the inexperienced spectator.

There is something between us, which Simenon has tried to convey without success, and that is, paradoxical as it may seem, a kind of family feeling.

Don't misunderstand me. We are on different sides of the barricade, of course. But we also, to some extent, share the same hardships.

The prostitute on the Boulevard de Clichy and the policeman who is watching her both have bad shoes and both have aching feet from trudging along miles of asphalt. They have to endure the same rain, the same icy wind. Evening and night wear the same hue for both of them, and they see with almost identical eyes the seamy side of the crowd that streams past them.

The same is true of a fair where a pickpocket is threading his way through a similar crowd. For him a fair, or indeed any gathering of some few hundreds of people, means not fun, roundabouts, Big Tops or gingerbread, but merely a certain number of purses in unwary pockets.

For the policeman too. And each of them can recognise at a glance the self-satisfied country visitor who will be the ideal victim.

How many times have I spent hours following a certain pickpocket of my acquaintance, such as the one we called the Artful Dodger! He knew that I was on his heels, watching his slightest movements. He knew that I knew. While I knew that he knew that I was there.

His job was to get hold of a wallet or a watch in spite of it all, and my job was to stop him or to catch him in the act.

Well, it sometimes happened that the Dodger would turn round and smile at me. I would smile back. He even spoke to me sometimes, with a sigh :

'It's going to be hard !'

I was well aware that he was on his beam-ends and that he wouldn't eat that night unless he was successful.

He was equally well aware that I earned a hundred francs a month, that I had holes in my shoes and that my wife was waiting impatiently for me at home.

Ten times at least I picked him up, quite kindly, telling him :

'You've had it !'

And he was almost as relieved as I was. It meant that

he'd get something to eat at the police station and somewhere to sleep. Some of them know the lock-up so well
that they ask :

'Who's on duty tonight ?'

Because some of us let them smoke and others don't.

Then, for a year and a half, the pavements seemed to
me an ideal beat, for my next job was in the big stores.

Instead of rain and cold, sunshine and dust, I spent my
days in an overheated atmosphere reeking of tweed and
unbleached calico, linoleum and mercerised cotton.

In those days there were radiators at intervals in the
gangways between counters, which sent up puffs of dry,
scorching air. This was fine when you arrived soaking
wet. You took up your position above a radiator, and
immediately you gave out a cloud of steam.

After a few hours, you chose rather to hang about near
the doors which, each time they opened, let in a little
oxygen.

The important thing was to look natural. To look like a
customer ! Which is so easy, isn't it, when the whole floor
is full of nothing but corsets, lingerie or reels of silk ?

'May I ask you to come along with me quietly ?'

Some women used to understand immediately and
followed us without a word to the manager's office. Others
got on their high horse, protested shrilly or had hysterics.

And yet here, too, we had to deal with a regular clientèle. Whether at the Bon Marché, the Louvre or the
Printemps, certain familiar figures were always to be
found, usually middle-aged women, who stowed away

incredible quantities of various goods in a pocket concealed between their dress and their petticoat.

A year and a half, in retrospect, seems very little, but at the time each hour was as long drawn out as an hour spent in the dentist's waiting-room.

'Shall you be at the Galeries this afternoon?' my wife would ask me sometimes. 'I've got a few little things to buy there.'

We never spoke to one another. We pretended not to recognise each other. It was delightful. I was happy to watch her moving proudly from one counter to the next, giving me a discreet wink from time to time.

I don't believe that she ever asked herself either whether she might have married anyone other than a police inspector. She knew the names of all my colleagues, spoke familiarly about those whom she had never seen, of their fads, of their successes or their failures.

It took me years to bring myself, one Sunday morning when I was on duty, to take her into the famous house in the Quai des Orfèvres, and she showed no sign of amazement. She walked about as if she were at home, looking for all the details which she knew so well from hearsay.

Her only reaction was :

'It's less dirty than I'd expected.'

'Why should it be dirty?'

'Places where men live by themselves are never quite so clean. And they have a certain smell.'

I did not ask her to the Police Station, where she'd have got her fill of smells.

'Who sits here on the left?'

'Torrence.'

'The big fat one? I might have guessed it. He's like a child. He still plays at carving his initials on his desk.'

'And what about old Lagrume, the man who walks so much?'

Since I've talked about shoes I may as well tell the story that distressed my wife.

Lagrume, Old Lagrume as we called him, was senior to all of us, although he had never risen above the rank of sergeant. He was a tall, melancholy fellow. In summer he suffered from hay-fever and, as soon as the weather turned cold, his chronic bronchitis gave him a hollow cough that sounded from one end of Headquarters to the other.

Fortunately he was not often there. He had been rash enough to say one day, referring to his cough:

'The doctor recommends me to keep in the open-air.'

After that, he got his fill of open-air. He had long legs and huge feet, and he was put in charge of the most un-likely investigations through the length and breadth of Paris, the sort that force you to travel through the town in all directions, day after day, without even the hope of getting any results.

'Just leave it to Lagrume!'

Everybody knew what was involved, except the old fellow himself, who gravely made a few notes on his pad, tucked his rolled umbrella under his arm and went off, with a brief nod to all present.

I wonder now whether he was not perfectly well aware of the part he was playing. He was one of the meek. For years and years he had had a sick wife waiting for him to do the housework in their suburban home. And when his daughter married, I believe it was he who got up at night to look after the baby :

'Lagrume, you still smell of dirty nappies !'

An old woman had been murdered in the Rue Caulaincourt. It was a commonplace crime that made no sensation in the Press, for the victim was an unimportant small *rentière* with no connections.

Such cases are always the most difficult. I myself, being confined to the big stores – and particularly busy as Christmas drew near – was not involved in it, but, like everybody else at our place, I knew the details of the investigation.

The crime had been committed with a kitchen knife, which had been left on the spot. This knife provided the only evidence. It was quite an ordinary knife, such as are sold in ironmongers' shops, chain stores or the smallest local shops, and the manufacturer, who had been contacted, claimed to have sold tens of thousands within the area of Paris.

The knife was a new one. It had obviously been bought on purpose. It still bore the price written on the handle in indelible pencil.

This was the detail which offered a vague hope of discovering the tradesman who had sold it.

'Lagrume ! You deal with that knife.'

He wrapped it up in a bit of newspaper, put it in his pocket and set off.

He set off for a journey through Paris which was to last for nine weeks.

Every morning he appeared punctually at the office, to which he would return in the evening to shut away the knife in a drawer. Every morning he was to be seen putting the weapon in his pocket, seizing his umbrella and setting out with the same nod to all present.

I learned the number of shops – the story has become a legend – which might possibly have sold a knife of this sort. Without going beyond the fortifications, and confining oneself to the twenty arrondissements of Paris, the number makes your head reel.

There was no question of using any means of transport. It meant going from street to street, almost from door to door. Lagrume had in his pocket a map of Paris on which, hour after hour, he crossed out a certain number of streets.

I believe that in the end his chiefs had even forgotten what task he had been set.

'Is Lagrume available?'

Somebody would reply that he was out on a job, and then nobody bothered any more about him. It was shortly before Christmas, as I have said. It was a wet, cold winter, the pavements were slimy, and yet Lagrume went to and fro from morning till night, with his bronchitis and his hollow cough, unwearying, never asking what was the point of it all.

During the ninth week, well into the New Year, when it

was freezing hard, he turned up at three o'clock in the afternoon, as calm and mournful as ever, without the slightest gleam of joy or relief in his eyes.

'Is the Chief there?'

'You've found it?'

'I've found it.'

Not in an ironmonger's, nor a cheap store, nor a household goods shop. He had gone through all those unavailingly.

The knife had been sold by a stationer in the Boulevard Rochechouart. The shopkeeper had recognised his handwriting, and remembered a young man in a green scarf buying the weapon from him more than two months previously.

He gave a fairly detailed description of him, and the young man was arrested and executed the following year.

As for Lagrume, he died in the street, not from his bronchitis but from a heart attack.

.    .    .

Before discussing stations, and in particular that Gare du Nord with which I always feel I have an old score to settle, I must deal briefly with a subject of which I am not very fond.

I have often been asked, with reference to my early days and my various jobs:

'Have you been in the Vice Squad too?'

It isn't known by that name today. It is modestly called the 'Social Squad.'

Well, I've belonged to that, like most of my colleagues. For a very short period. Barely a few months.

And if I realise now that it was necessary, my recollections of that period are nevertheless confused and somewhat uneasy.

I mentioned the familiarity that grows up naturally between policemen and those on whom it is their job to keep watch.

By force of circumstances, it exists in that branch as much as in the others. Even more so. Indeed, the *clientèle* of each detective, so to speak, consists of a relatively restricted number of women who are almost always found at the same spots, at the door of the same hotel or under the same street lamp, or, for the grade above, at the terrace of the same brasseries.

I was not then as stalwart as I have grown with the passing years, and apparently I looked younger than my age.

Remember the *petits fours* incident at the Boulevard Beaumarchais and you will understand that in certain respects I was somewhat timid.

Most of the officers in the Vice Squad were on familiar terms with the women, whose names or nicknames they knew, and it was a tradition when, during the course of a raid, they packed them into the Black Maria, to vie with one another in coarseness of speech, to fling the filthiest abuse at one another with a laugh.

Another habit these ladies had acquired was to pick up their skirts and show their behinds in a gesture which they considered, no doubt, the last word in insults, and which they accompanied with a torrent of defiance.

I must have blushed to begin with, for I still blushed easily. My embarrassment did not pass unnoticed, for the least one can say of these women is that they have a certain knowledge of men.

I promptly became, not exactly their *bête noire*, but their butt.

At the Quai des Orfèvres nobody ever called me by my first name, and I'm convinced that many of my colleagues did not know it . . . I shouldn't have chosen it if I'd been asked my opinion. I'm not ashamed of it either.

Could it have been some sly revenge on the part of some detective who was in the know?

I was specially in charge of the Sébastopol district which, particularly in the Halles area, was frequented at that time by the lowest class of women, particularly by a number of very old prostitutes who had taken refuge there.

It was here, too, that young servant girls newly arrived from Brittany or elsewhere served their apprenticeship, so that one had the two extremes: kids of sixteen, over whom the pimps quarrelled, and ancient harpies who were very well able to defend themselves.

One day the catchphrase started – for it quickly became a catchphrase. I was walking past one of these old women, stationed at the door of a filthy hotel, when I heard her call out to me, showing all her rotten teeth in a smile :

'Good evening, Jules !'

I thought she'd used the name at random, but a little further on I was greeted by the same words.

'Hullo, Jules!'

After which, when there was a group of them together, they would burst out laughing, with a flood of unrepeatable comments.

I know what some officers would have done in my place. They'd have needed no further inducement to pick up a few of these women and lock them up at Saint-Lazare to think things over.

The example would have served its purpose, and I should probably have been treated with a certain respect.

I didn't do it. Not necessarily from any sense of justice. Nor out of pity.

Probably because this was a game I didn't want to play. I chose rather to pretend I hadn't heard. I hoped they would tire of it. But such women are like children who have never had enough of any joke.

They made up a song about Jules which they began to sing or yell as soon as I appeared. Others would say to me, as I checked their cards:

'Don't be mean, Jules! You're so sweet!'

Poor Louise! Her great dread, during this period, was not that I might yield to some temptation, but that I might bring home an unpleasant disease. Once I caught fleas. When I got home she would make me undress and take a bath, while she went to brush my clothes on the landing or at the open window.

'You must have touched plenty today! Brush your nails well!'

Wasn't there some story that you could catch syphilis merely by drinking out of a glass?

It was not a pleasant experience, but I learned what I had to learn. After all, I had chosen my own career.

For nothing on earth would I have asked to be transferred. My chiefs did what was necessary of their own accord, more for the sake of results, I imagine, than out of consideration for myself.

I was put on stations. More precisely, I was posted to that gloomy, sinister building known as the Gare du Nord.

.     .     .

It had the advantage, like the big stores, that one was sheltered from the rain. Not from the cold nor from the wind, for nowhere in the world, probably, are there so many draughts as in the hall of a station, the hall of the Gare du Nord, and for months I had as many colds as old Lagrume.

Please don't imagine that I'm grumbling, or deliberately dwelling on the seamy side so as to get my own back.

I was perfectly happy. I was happy trudging along the streets and I was equally happy keeping an eye on so-called kleptomaniacs in the big stores. I felt that I was getting on a little each time, learning a job whose complexity was more apparent to me every day.

When I see the Gare de l'Est, for instance, I can never

help feeling depressed, because it reminds me of mobiliza-
tion. The Gare de Lyon, on the other hand, like the Gare
Montparnasse, suggests holidays.

But the Gare du Nord, the coldest, the busiest of them
all, brings to my mind a harsh and bitter struggle for one's
daily bread. Is it because it leads towards mining and
industrial regions?

In the morning, the first night trains, coming from
Belgium and Germany, generally contain a certain number of smugglers, of illicit traders with faces as hard as
the daylight seen through the glazed windows of the
station.

It's not always a matter of small-scale fraud. There are
the professionals in various international rackets, with
their agents, their decoys, their right-hand men, people
who play for high stakes and are ready to defend themselves by any method.

No sooner has this crowd dispersed than it's the turn
of the suburban trains which come not from pleasant villages like those in the West or South, but from black,
unhealthy built-up areas.

In the opposite direction, it's towards Belgium, the
nearest frontier, that fugitives for the most varied reasons
try to escape.

Hundreds of people are waiting there in the grey atmosphere redolent of smoke and sweat, moving restlessly,
hurrying from the booking office to the waiting rooms,
examining the boards that announce arrivals and depar-
tures, eating or drinking, surrounded by children, dogs

and suitcases, and almost always they are people who have not slept enough, whose nerves are on edge from their dread of being late, sometimes merely from their dread of the morrow which they are going elsewhere to seek.

I have spent hours, every day, watching them, looking amongst all those faces for some more inscrutable face with a more fixed stare, the face of a man or woman staking their last chance.

The train is there, about to leave in a few minutes. He's only got to go another hundred yards and hold out the ticket he's clutching. The minute hands jerk forward on the enormous yellowish face of the clock.

Double or quits! It means freedom or jail. Or worse.

I am there, with a photograph or a description in my wallet, sometimes merely the technical description of an ear.

It may happen that we catch sight of one another simultaneously, that our eyes meet. Almost invariably the man understands at once.

What follows will depend on his character, on the risk he's running, on his nerves, even on some tiny material detail, a door that's open or shut, a trunk that may happen to be lying between us.

Sometimes they try to run away, and then there's a desperate race through groups of people who protest or try to get out of the way, a race among stationary coaches, over railway lines and points.

I have come across two men, one of them quite young,

who, at three months' distance, behaved in exactly the same way.

Each of them thrust his hand into his pocket as if to take out a cigarette. And next minute, in the thick of the crowd, with his eyes fixed on me, each of them shot himself through the head.

These men bore me no ill-will, nor did I bear them any. We were each of us doing his job.

They had lost the game, and there was an end to it, so they were quitting.

I had lost it too, for my duty was to bring them into the courts alive.

I have watched thousands of trains leaving. I have watched thousands arriving too, each time with the same dense crowd, the long string of people hurrying towards something or other.

It's become a habit with me, as with my colleagues. Even if I'm not on duty, if by some miracle I'm going on holiday with my wife, my glance slips from one face to the next, and seldom fails to fall on somebody who's afraid, however he may try to conceal it.

'Aren't you coming? What's the matter?'

Until we're settled in our carriage, or rather until the train has left, my wife is never sure that we're really going to get our holiday.

'What are you bothering about? You're not on duty!'

There have been times when I've followed her with a sigh, turning round for a last look at some mysterious face vanishing in the crowd. Always reluctantly.

And I don't think it's only from professional conscientiousness, nor from love of justice.

I repeat, it's a game that's being played, a game that has no end. Once you've begun it, it's difficult, if not impossible, to give it up.

The proof is that those of us who eventually retire, often against their will, almost always end by setting up a private detective agency.

Moreover that's only a last resort, and I don't know one detective who, after grumbling for thirty years about the miseries of a policeman's life, isn't ready to take up work again, even unpaid.

I have sinister memories of the Gare du Nord. I don't know why, I always picture it full of thick, damp early-morning fog, with its drowsy crowd flocking towards the lines or towards the Rue Maubeuge.

The specimens of humanity I have met there have been some of the most desperate, and certain arrests that I have made there left me with a feeling of remorse rather than of any professional satisfaction.

If I had the choice, none the less, I would rather go on duty again tomorrow at the platform barrier than set off from some more sumptuous station for a sunny corner of the Côte d'Azur.

# CHAPTER SIX

*One staircase after another!*

FROM time to time, almost always on the occasion of some political upheaval, troubles break out in the streets which are no longer merely the manifestation of popular discontent. It would seem that at a certain moment a breach is formed, invisible sluices are opened, and there suddenly appear in the wealthier districts creatures whose very existence is generally unknown there, who seem to have emerged from some haunt of beggars and whom the inhabitants watch from their windows as they might watch ruffians and cutthroats suddenly appearing from the depths of the Middle Ages.

What surprised me most, when this phenomenon occurred with notable violence after the riots on February 6th, was the astonishment expressed next day by most of the newspapers.

This invasion of the heart of Paris, for a few hours, not by demonstrators but by haggard individuals who spread as much terror around them as a pack of wolves, suddenly alarmed people who, by their profession, are almost as closely acquainted as ourselves with the underworld of a metropolis.

Paris was really frightened that time. Then, the very next day, once order was restored, Paris forgot that this rabble had not been destroyed, that it had simply gone to earth.

Of course, it's up to the police to keep it there.

Is it generally known that there is one squad solely concerned with the two to three hundred thousand North Africans, Portuguese and Algerians who live in the outskirts of the 20th arrondissement, who camp out there, one might rather say, scarcely knowing our language or not knowing it at all, obeying other laws, other reflexes than our own?

We have, at Headquarters, maps on which are marked little islands, as it were, in coloured pencil, the Jews of the Rue des Rosiers, the Italians of the Hôtel de Ville district, the Russians of Les Ternes and Denfert-Rochereau . . .

Many of them ask nothing better than to be assimilated, and our difficulties don't come from them, but there are some who, whether as a group or as individuals, keep deliberately on the fringe and lead their mysterious lives, unnoticed by the crowd around them.

Highly respectable people, whose petty frauds and meannesses are carefully camouflaged, are almost always the ones who ask me, with that slight quiver of the lips that I know so well :

'Aren't you sometimes disgusted?'

They aren't referring to any particular thing, but to the whole set of people we have to deal with. What they would like is to have us disclose really nasty secrets to them, unheard-of vices, a lot of filth at which they could express their horror while secretly relishing it.

Such people often use the term 'the dregs of society'.

'What dreadful things you must see among the dregs of society!'

I prefer not to answer them. I look at them in a certain way, without any expression on my face, and they must understand my meaning, for they generally look uncomfortable and don't ask any more.

I learned a great deal on the public highway. I learned much, too, on fairgrounds and in big stores, wherever crowds were gathered.

I have spoken of my experiences at the Gare du Nord.

But it was while I was in the Hotels Squad that I learned most about men, particularly those men who frighten the inhabitants of wealthy districts when the sluices happen to open.

Hobnailed shoes were no longer needed here, for one's job was not to cover miles of pavement but to trudge in a vertical direction, so to speak.

Every day I collected the index cards of some tens of hundreds of hotels, usually furnished apartment houses, where there was seldom a lift and one had to climb six or seven floors up a stifling staircase, amid a sickeningly acrid smell of poverty-stricken humanity.

Big hotels with revolving doors flanked by liveried servants have their own dramas too, their secrets into which the police pry daily.

But it's chiefly in thousands of hotels with unfamiliar names, inconspicuous from outside, that a certain floating population goes to earth, a population which is difficult to get hold of elsewhere and seldom law-abiding. We went in couples. Sometimes, in dangerous districts, we went in larger groups. We would choose the time at which most people were in bed, shortly after midnight.

Then a sort of nightmare would begin, with certain details always recurring, the night watchman, the land-lord or his wife lying in bed behind the wicket and waking up unwillingly to try and forestall any accusation.

'You know quite well we've never had any trouble here . . .'

In old days the names used to be written in registers. Later, when identity cards became compulsory, there were forms to be filled in.

One of us would stay below. The other went upstairs. Sometimes we were spotted in spite of all our precautions, and from the ground floor we would hear the house be-ginning to stir like a beehive, busy comings and goings in the rooms, furtive footsteps on the stairs.

Occasionally we would find a room empty, the bed still warm, and at the top of the house the skylight that gave on to the roofs would be open.

Usually we managed to reach the first floor without rousing the lodgers, and we would knock at the first door and be answered by grunts, by questions almost invariably in a foreign language.

'Police!'

That's a word they all understand. And then, in their underclothes or stark naked, men, women and children scurry about in the dim light, in the stench, unfastening unbelievable cases to hunt for a passport hidden under their belongings.

There's no describing the anxious look in those eyes, those sleepwalker's movements, and that particular brand of humility which is found only in the uprooted. A proud humility, shall I call it?

They did not hate us. We were the masters. We had – or they believed we had – the most terrible of all powers: that of sending them back across the frontier.

For some of them the fact of being here represented years of scheming or waiting. They had reached the promised land. They owned papers, real or forged.

And while they held them out to us, fearful lest we should thrust them in our pockets, they tried instinctively to win us with a smile, found a few words of French to stammer:

'Please, Mister Officer . . .'

The women rarely bothered about decency, and sometimes you would see a hesitant look in their eyes, and they would make a vague gesture towards the tumbled bed. Weren't we tempted? wouldn't we like to?

And yet all these people had their pride, a special pride that I cannot describe. The pride of wild animals?

Indeed, it was rather like caged beasts that they watched us pass, without knowing whether we were going to strike them or stroke them.

Sometimes you'd see one of them brandishing his papers, panic-stricken, and he'd start talking volubly in his own language, gesticulating, calling the rest to his aid, striving to make us believe that he was an honest man, that appearances were misleading, that ...

Some would start weeping and others crouched sullenly in their corner as if they were about to spring, though actually resigned.

Identity check-up. That's what the operation is called in administrative language. Those whose papers are indisputably in order are allowed to stay in their rooms, where you hear them lock the door with a sigh of relief.

The others ...

'Come downstairs!'

When they don't understand, you have to add a gesture. And they get dressed, talking to themselves. They don't know what they ought to take, or are allowed to take with them. Occasionally, as soon as our backs are turned, they slip back to get some hidden treasure and thrust it into their pockets or under their shirts.

They all stand about on the ground floor in a small silent group, each thinking only of his own case and how he's going to defend himself.

In the Saint-Antoine district there are certain hotels where I have found up to seven or eight Poles in a single room, most of them sleeping on the floor.

Only one was inscribed on the register. Did the landlord know? Did he exact payment for the additional sleepers? It's more than likely, but it's useless to try and prove such things.

The others' papers, needless to say, were not in order.

What did they do when they had to leave the shelter of the room at daybreak?

For lack of work-cards, they could not earn a regular living. But they had not died of starvation. So they must have been eating somehow.

And there were, and still are, thousands, tens of thousands in the same case.

You may find money in their pockets, or hidden on top of some cupboard, or more frequently in their shoes. Then you have to discover how they procured it, and that's the most exhausting kind of cross-examination.

Even if they understand French they pretend not to understand it. Looking you in the eyes with an expression of good will, indefatigably reasserting their innocence.

It's useless to ask the others about them. They never betray one another. They will all tell the same story.

Now, on an average, sixty-five per cent of the crimes committed in the Paris area are due to foreigners.

Stairs, stairs and yet more stairs. Not only by night but by day, and tarts everywhere, professionals and others, some of them young and fine-looking, come, God knows why, from the depths of their own country.

I knew one of these, a Polish woman, who shared a hotel room in the Rue Saint-Antoine with five men, whom she used to send out on robberies, rewarding those who were successful in her own fashion, while the others fretted impatiently in the same room and afterwards usually fell savagely upon the exhausted winner.

Two of them were enormous powerful brutes, and she

was not afraid of them, she could hold them in awe with a smile or a frown; while I was questioning them, in my own office, after some remark or other made in their own language I saw her calmly slap one of these giants in the face.

'You must see a queer lot of things!'

Well, we see men and women, all sorts of men and women in the most unbelievable situations, at every social level. We see them, we take note and we try to understand.

I don't mean understand some deep human mystery or other. That romantic idea is possibly the thing against which I protest the most earnestly, almost angrily. This is one of the reasons for this book, for these attempted corrections. Simenon has endeavoured to explain this, I admit. Nevertheless I have felt a certain embarrassment on seeing attributed to myself in his books certain smiles, certain attitudes which I have never assumed and which would have made my colleagues shrug their shoulders.

The person who has understood things best is my wife. And yet when I get back from work she never questions me with any curiosity, whatever the case with which I am concerned.

For my part, I don't deliberately take her into my confidence.

I sit down at table like any other official coming home from work. In a few words, as though for my own benefit, I may describe an encounter, an interview, or talk of the man or woman about whom I am making investigations.

If she puts a question, it's almost always a technical one.

'In which district?'

Or else:

'How old?'

Or again:

'How long has she been in France?'

For she has come to consider such details as revealing as we have ourselves.

She does not question me about sordid or pathetic side-issues.

And Heaven knows it's not for lack of feeling!

'Has his wife been to see him at the Police Station?'

'This morning.'

'Did she take the child with her?'

She takes a particular interest, for reasons on which I need not enlarge, in those who have children, and it would be a mistake to fancy that law-breakers, malefactors and criminals have none.

We had one of these in our own home, a little girl whose mother I had sent to prison for life, but we knew that the father would take her back as soon as he was restored to normal life.

She still comes to see us. She is a grown girl now, and my wife takes pride in going round the shops with her in the afternoon.

What I want to stress is that our behaviour towards those with whom we have to deal involved neither sentimentality nor hardness, neither hatred nor pity in the usual sense of the word.

Our job is to study men. We watch their behaviour. We take note of some of the facts. We try to establish others.

When, as a young man, I had to visit a disreputable lodging house from cellar to attic, exploring rooms like cells in a honeycomb, surprising people in their sleep, in their most elementary privacy, examining their papers through a magnifying glass, I could almost have foretold what would become of each of them.

For one thing, certain faces were already familiar to me, for Paris is not so big that one doesn't constantly come across the same individuals, in a given environment.

Certain cases, too, recur almost identically, the same causes producing the same results.

The wretched Central European who had saved for months, if not years, to buy himself false passports from a clandestine agency in his own country, and who thought his troubles were over once he had safely crossed the frontier, will inevitably fall into our hands before six months, or twelve at most, are out.

Indeed, we could even follow him in our mind's eye from the frontier, and foretell in what district, in what restaurant, in what lodging house he will end up.

We know through whom he will try to procure the indispensable labour permit, genuine or forged; we shall merely have to go and pick him up in the queue that stretches out every morning in front of the big factories at Javel.

Why should we feel anger or resentment, when he lands up where he was bound to land up?

The same thing happens with the fresh-faced servant girl whom we see paying her first visit to a certain dance hall. Can we tell her to go back to her employers and keep away from that flashy companion of hers?

It would do no good. She'll come back. We shall meet her at other dance halls, then, one fine evening, outside the door of some hotel in the Halles or Bastille district.

Ten thousand go that way on an average, every year, ten thousand who leave their village and start off in domestic service in Paris, and who before a few months or a few weeks are out will have taken the plunge.

Is it so very different when a boy of eighteen or twenty, who has been working in a factory, begins to dress in a certain way, to adopt certain poses, to lean on the zinc counters of certain bars?

We shall see him presently in a new suit, wearing artificial silk socks and tie.

He'll end up in our hands too, looking shifty or crestfallen, after an attempted burglary or smash and grab raid, unless he has joined the car thieves' brigade.

There are certain signs you cannot mistake, and it was really these signs which we were learning to recognise when we were sent to serve in every squad in turn, to cover miles of pavement on foot, climb up stair after stair and make our way into every sort of hovel and amidst every type of crowd.

That was why the nickname 'hobnailed socks' never annoyed us, quite the reverse.

There are few of us at Headquarters who, by the time they are forty, aren't well acquainted, for instance, with all the pickpockets. We even know where to find them on such and such a day, on the occasion of such and such a ceremony or festivity.

In the same way we know, for instance, that there will shortly be a jewel robbery, because a certain specialist who has seldom been caught redhanded has begun to run short of cash. He has left his hotel in the Boulevard Haussmann for a humbler one in the République district. He hasn't paid his bill for a fortnight. The woman with whom he's living has begun to have rows with him, and has bought no new hats for a long time.

We cannot follow him step by step; there would never be enough detectives to shadow every suspect. But we have him on the end of a string. The Public Highways Squad have been warned to keep a special eye on jewellers' shops. We know his way of working. We know he'll never work any other way.

It doesn't always come off. That would be too much to hope for. But it sometimes happens that he's caught in the act. It sometimes happens after a discreet interview with his girl friend, who's been given the hint that her own future would be less problematic if she provided us with information.

The papers talk a great deal about gangs settling accounts with one another in Montmartre or the area round the Rue Fontaine, because there's always something exciting for the public about revolver shots by night.

But those are just the cases that worry us least at Headquarters.

We know the rival gangs, their interests and the points at issue between them. We also know their personal hatreds and resentments.

One crime calls forth another, by repercussion. If someone shoots down Luciano in a bar in the Rue de Douai, the Corsicans will inevitably take their revenge before very long. And almost always there's one amongst them who will give us the hint.

'Something's being plotted against Flatfooted Dédé. He knows it and he won't go out without a couple of killers as bodyguard.'

The day when Dédé gets his, it's ninety per cent certain that a more or less mysterious telephone call will put us in the picture about every detail of the story.

'There's one the less!'

We do arrest the guilty men, but it really makes little difference, for those people only exterminate one another, for reasons of their own, according to a certain code which they apply strictly.

It was to this that Simenon was alluding when, during our first interview, he declared so categorically:

'Professional crimes don't interest me.'

What he did not know then, but has learnt since, is that there are very few other sorts of crime.

I'm not including crimes of passion, which are straightforward for the most part, being merely the logical issue of an acute crisis between two or more individuals.

I'm not including those brawls where a couple of drunks knife one another one Saturday or Sunday night in the slums.

Apart from such accidents, the most frequent crimes are of two sorts :

The murder of some lonely old woman by one or more hooligans, and the murder of a prostitute in some piece of waste ground.

In the first case the culprit rarely escapes. Almost always he is one of those youngsters I mentioned before, who quit factory work a few months back, and is dying to show off his toughness.

He's had his eye on some tobacconist's or haberdasher's, some small shop in a quiet back-street.

Sometimes he's bought a revolver. At other times he makes do with a hammer or spanner.

Almost invariably he knows his victim and, in at least one case out of ten, she has done him a kindness at some time or another.

He has not planned to kill. He's put a scarf over his face so as not to be recognised.

The scarf slips, or else the old woman begins to scream.

He fires. He strikes. If he fires he empties the whole barrel, which is a sign of panic. If he strikes he strikes ten or twenty blows, savagely so it seems, but really because he's crazy with terror.

Does it surprise you that when we've got him in front

of us, in a state of collapse and yet still trying to swagger, we merely say to him :

'You fool !'

They almost always pay with their lives. The least they can get away with is twenty years, when they're lucky enough to interest some first-rate counsel.

As for the murderers of prostitutes, it's only by a miracle that we lay hands on them. These investigations are the longest, the most discouraging, the most sickening I know.

They usually begin with a sack being fished up by some waterman on the end of his boathook, somewhere along the Seine, and containing, almost always, a mutilated body. The head is missing, or an arm, or both legs.

Weeks go by before identification is possible. Generally the victim is one of these elderly whores who don't even take their customers to a hotel or to their room, but make do with some doorway or the shelter of a railing.

She hadn't been seen lately in her neighbourhood, one of those districts which, as soon as night falls, becomes full of mystery and silent shadows.

The women who knew her are not anxious to get into contact with us. When we question them they give only the vaguest answers.

Eventually, by dint of patience, we manage, after a fashion, to discover some of her usual clients, lonely individuals themselves, solitary men of indefinite age who are remembered merely as shadowy figures.

Was she killed for her money? It's hardly likely. She had so little ! Had one of these old fellows suddenly gone crazy, or did someone come from elsewhere, from another district, one of those maniacs who at regular intervals feel a fit coming on, know exactly what they will do and with incredible lucidity take precautions of which other criminals are incapable?

No one knows how many there are of these. There are some in every capital city, and, once the deed is done, they disappear once more, for a greater or less length of time, into anonymity.

They may be respectable people, fathers of families, model employees.

Nobody knows exactly what they're like, and when by chance we catch one of them it has almost always been impossible to establish a satisfactory conviction.

We possess more or less exact statistics for crimes of every sort.

Except one.

Poisoning.

And any rough guess would inevitably err in one direction or the other.

Every three months, or six months, in Paris or in the provinces, particularly in the provinces, in some very small town or in the country, a doctor may happen by chance to examine a dead body more closely than usual and be puzzled by certain symptoms.

I say chance, for the dead man is usually one of his patients, somebody he has known to be ill for a long time. The man has died suddenly, in his bed, in the bosom of his family, who display all the traditional signs of grief.

The relations dislike the suggestion of an autopsy. The doctor only insists on one if his suspicions are strong enough.

Or else, weeks after the funeral, an anonymous letter reaches the police, providing details which at first sight seem incredible.

I stress this to show all the circumstances that must be combined before such an investigation can be held. The administrative formalities are complicated.

The commonest case is that of a farmer's wife who has been waiting for years for her husband to die in order to set up house with the farm hand, and who has lost patience.

She has come to the help of Nature, as some people crudely put it.

Sometimes, though more rarely, a man will use the same method to get rid of an ailing wife who has become a dead weight in his home.

They are found out by chance. But how many other cases are there where chance does not play its part? We don't know. We can only risk hypotheses. There are some of us at Headquarters, as there are in the Rue des Saussaies, who believe that of all crimes, particularly of those that go unpunished, this particular sort is the most frequent.

The others, those that interest novelists and so-called psychologists, are so unusual that they absorb only an insignificant part of our activities.

But that is the part with which the public is most

familiar. These are the cases about which Simenon has written most and will, I suppose, go on writing.

I refer to those crimes which are committed suddenly in the most unlikely settings, and which are, as it were, the final outcome of something that has been brewing for a long time in secret.

Some well-kept, prosperous street in Paris or elsewhere. People who have a comfortable house, a family life, an honourable profession.

We have never had occasion to cross their threshold. Often the *milieu* is one to which we should normally not have access, where our presence would jar, where we should feel awkward, to say the least.

Now somebody has died a violent death, and so we come and ring at the door, and find ourselves confronted by inscrutable faces, by a family of which each member seems to have his own secret.

Here the experience acquired through years in streets, in stations, in lodging houses is no longer involved. Nor is that sort of instinctive respect felt by small fry towards authority, towards the police.

Nobody here is afraid of being sent back over the frontier. Nobody is going to be taken off to an office at Headquarters to be subjected for hours to a painstaking examination, gone over again and again.

The people we have before us are those highly respectable folk who in other circumstances would have asked us :

'Don't you sometimes feel disgusted?'

We do, in these very homes. Not immediately. Not invariably. For the task is a long and chancy one.

Even when a telephone call from some minister, some deputy, some important public figure doesn't try to divert us from our path.

There is a whole varnish of respectability to be peeled off little by little; there are family secrets, more or less repulsive, which they all combine to conceal from us and which have to be brought to light, regardless of protests and threats.

Sometimes five or six of them, or more, may have conspired to lie on certain points, while surreptitiously endeavouring to get the rest into trouble.

Simenon is apt to describe me as awkward and gruff, feeling ill at ease, with a furtive glance and a cantankerous way of barking out my questions.

It's in such cases as these that he has seen me thus, faced with what one might call amateur crimes, which one *invariably* discovers, in the end, to have been committed for motives of self-interest.

Not for money. I mean not crimes committed from an urgent need for money, as in the case of those petty ruffians who murder old women.

The interests involved behind these façades are more complicated, they are long-term interests, coupled with a concern for respectability. Often the thing goes back many years, concealing a whole lifetime of intrigue and dishonesty.

When these people, brought to bay, finally confess, the

whole revolting story comes out, almost always with a panic fear of consequences.

'Surely it's impossible for our family to be dragged in the mud? There must be some way out.'

That does happen, I'm sorry to say. Some people who should only have left my office for a cell at the Santé prison have disappeared from circulation, because there are certain influences against which a detective, even a chief-inspector, is powerless.

'Don't you sometimes feel disgusted?'

I have never done so when, as detective in the Hotels Squad, I spent my days or my nights climbing the stairs of squalid, overcrowded apartment houses, where every door disclosed some distressing or dramatic scene.

Nor does the word disgust convey my reaction to the thousands of professionals of every sort who have passed through my hands.

They have played their game and lost it. Almost all of them prided themselves on being good losers and some of them, after they had been sentenced, asked me to go and see them in prison, where we chatted like old friends.

I could mention several who have begged me to be present at their execution and saved their last dying look for me.

'I shall do all right, you'll see!'

They did their best. They were not always successful. I used to take away their last letters in my pocket, promising to send them off with a covering note of my own.

When I got home, my wife had only to look at me

without asking questions to know how things had gone off.

As for the other cases, on which I prefer not to dwell, she was well acquainted with the meaning of certain angry moods of mine, a certain way of sitting down when I got home at night, and of filling my plate, and she never pressed me.

Which is ample proof that she was not destined for the Highways and Bridges!

# CHAPTER SEVEN

*Describes a morning as triumphant as a cavalry trumpet
and a young fellow who was no longer thin, but who
had not yet grown really stout.*

I CAN still recall the taste and the colour of the sunlight
that morning. It was in March. Spring had come early. I
had already formed the habit of going on foot, whenever
I could, from the Boulevard Richard-Lenoir to the Quai
des Orfèvres.

I had no outside work that day, only files to classify in
the Hotels section, in what were probably the gloomiest
offices in the whole Palais de Justice, on the ground floor,
with a little door leading into the courtyard, which I had
left open.

I kept as near to it as my work allowed. I remember the
sun cutting the courtyard exactly in two, and also cutting
across a waiting police van. From time to time its two
horses stamped on the paving-stones, and behind them
there was a fine heap of gleaming dung, smoking in the
keen morning air.

I don't know why the courtyard reminded me of certain break-times at school, at the same season of the year,
when the air suddenly begins to have a special fragrance
and, when you've been running, your skin smells of spring.

I was alone in the office. The telephone bell rang.

'Will you tell Maigret the Chief wants him?'

The voice of the old office clerk up there, who had been nearly fifty years in his job.

'Maigret speaking.'

'Come up then.'

Even the great staircase, which was always full of dust, seemed gay, with rays of sunlight slanting down as in churches. The morning conference had just ended. Two inspectors still stood talking, with their files under their arms, by the Chief's door, on which I went to knock.

And inside the office I could still smell the pipes and cigarettes of those who had just gone out. A window was open behind Xavier Guichard, who had plumes of sunlight in his silky white hair.

He did not hold out his hand to me. He seldom did so in the office. And yet we had become friends, or, more precisely, he had been good enough to honour my wife and me with his friendship. On one occasion, the first, he had invited me alone to his flat in the Boulevard Saint-Germain. Not the wealthy, fashionable part of the Boulevard. He lived, on the contrary, right opposite the Place Maubert, in a big new block that rose amidst rickety houses and squalid hotels.

I had gone back there with my wife. They had immediately got on very well together.

He was undoubtedly fond of her and of myself, and yet he has often hurt us without meaning to.

In the beginning, as soon as he saw Louise, he would stare insistently at her figure and, if we seemed not to understand, he would say with a little cough:

'Don't forget that I want to be godfather.'

He was a confirmed bachelor. Apart from his brother, who was Chief of the Municipal Police, he had no relatives in Paris.

'Come now, don't keep me waiting too long . . .'

Years had gone by. He must have misunderstood. I remember that when he told me of my first rise he had added :

'Perhaps that'll enable you to give me a godson.'

He never understood why we blushed, why my wife lowered her eyes, while I tried to touch her hand to comfort her.

He was looking very serious that morning, seen against the light. He left me standing, and I felt embarrassed by the insistent way in which he examined me from head to foot, as a sergeant-major looks over a recruit.

'D'you know, Maigret, you're putting on weight?'

I was thirty. Little by little I had stopped being thin, my shoulders had broadened, my chest had expanded, but I had not yet become really stout.

It was obvious. I must have seemed flabby in those days, with a somewhat babyish look. It struck me myself when I passed in front of a shop window and cast an anxious glance at my own silhouette.

It was too much or too little, and no clothes fitted me.

'I think I'm getting fatter, yes.'

I almost wanted to apologise and I had not yet realised that he was joking as he loved to do :

'I think I'd better transfer you to another department.'

There were two squads in which I had not yet served, the Sports Squad and the Finance Squad, and the latter was my nightmare, just as the trigonometry exam had long been the terror of my summer terms at school.

'How old are you?'

'Thirty.'

'The right age! That's fine. Young Lesueur will take your place in the Hotels Squad, from now on, and you shall put yourself at Inspector Guillaume's disposal.'

He deliberately said this in an unemphatic tone, as if it were something quite trivial, knowing that my heart was going to leap in my breast and that, as I stood before him there, I could hear triumphant clarion calls ringing in my ears.

Suddenly, on a morning that seemed to have been chosen on purpose – and I'm not sure that Guichard hadn't done so – the dream of my life was being realised.

At last I was to enter the Special Squad.

A quarter of an hour later I moved upstairs with my old office jacket, my soap and towel, my pencils and a few papers.

There were five or six men in the big room reserved for Detectives in the Homicide Squad, and before calling me, Inspector Guillaume let me settle down, like a new pupil.

'Stand us a drink on it?'

I wasn't going to say no. At midday I proudly took my new colleagues to the Brasserie Dauphine.

I had often seen them there, at a different table from the one I shared with my former pals, and we used to watch them with the envious respect felt by schoolboys for sixth formers who are as tall as their masters and treated by these almost on an equal footing.

The comparison was an apt one, for Guillaume was with us, and the Superintendent from the General Information Department came to join us.

'What'll you have?' I asked.

In our old corner we used to drink half-pints of beer, seldom an apéritif. Obviously that wouldn't do for this table.

Somebody said :

'A mandarin-curaçao.'

'Mandarins all round?'

As nobody objected, I ordered I don't know how many mandarins. It was the first time I had tasted one. In the intoxication of my triumph, it seemed to me barely alcoholic.

'Let's have another round.'

Wasn't this the moment, if ever, to show myself generous? We had three each, we had four. My new Chief insisted on paying his round too.

The town was full of sunlight. The streets were streaming with it. The women in their bright dresses were a delight. I threaded my way between pedestrians. I looked at myself in shop windows and thought I wasn't so fat after all.

I ran. I flew. I was exultant. As soon as I reached the foot of the stairs I began the speech I had prepared for my wife.

Going up the last flight, I came a cropper. I hadn't had time to get up again when our door opened, for Louise must have been getting anxious at my delay.

'Have you hurt yourself?'

It was a funny thing. At the precise moment when I stood up again I felt completely drunk and was amazed at it. The staircase was whirling round me. My wife's silhouette was blurred. She seemed to have at least two mouths and three or four eyes.

Believe it or not, it was the first time in my life that this had happened to me, and I felt so humiliated that I dared not look at her; I slunk into the flat like a guilty thing without remembering the triumphant phrases I had so carefully prepared.

'I think . . . I think I'm a bit drunk.'

I was painfully sniffling. The table was laid, with our two places opposite one another in front of the open window. I had promised myself to take her out to lunch at a restaurant, but I dared not propose it now.

So that it was in an almost gloomy tone that I announced:

'It's happened!'

'What's happened?'

Perhaps she was expecting me to tell her that I'd been flung out of the Force!

'I've been appointed.'

'Appointed what?'

Apparently I had great tears in my eyes, tears of vexation but also, no doubt, of joy, as I let fall the words:

'To the Special Squad.'

'Sit down. I'm going to make you a cup of strong black coffee.'

She tried to get me to lie down, but I was not going to desert my new post on the first day. I drank I don't know how many cups of strong coffee. In spite of Louise's insistence I couldn't swallow any solid food. I took a shower.

At two o'clock, when I went along to the Quai des Orfèvres, my cheeks had a peculiar rosy glow, my eyes were glittering. I felt limp and light-headed.

I went to sit down in my corner and spoke as little as possible, for I knew that my voice was unsteady and that I might get my syllables confused.

Next day, as though to put me to the test, they entrusted me with my first arrest. It was in the Rue du Roi de Sicile, in an apartment house. The man had been shadowed for five days already. He was responsible for several murders. He was a foreigner, a Czech if I remember rightly, a strongly-built fellow, invariably armed, invariably on the alert.

The problem was to immobilise him before he had time to defend himself, for he was the sort of man who would fire into the crowd, kill as many people as possible before letting himself be brought down.

He knew that he was at the end of his tether, that the police were on his heels but were still hesitating.

Out of doors he always managed to stay in the middle of a crowd, well aware that we could take no risks.

I was sent as assistant to Inspector Dufour, who had

been following the man for several days and knew all his movements.

This was the first time, too, that I disguised myself. To have appeared in that sordid hotel dressed as we usually were would have provoked a panic under cover of which our man might have escaped.

Dufour and I put on old clothes and, to make things more convincing, went forty-eight hours without shaving.

A young detective, a skilled locksmith, had got into the hotel and had made us an excellent key of the man's bedroom.

We took a room on the same landing ourselves, before the Czech came back to bed. It was just after eleven when a signal from outside warned us that he was coming up the stairs.

The tactics we followed were not suggested by myself but by Dufour, an old hand at the game.

The man, not far away from us, had shut his door and was lying fully clothed on his bed, and he probably had a loaded revolver at least within reach.

We did not sleep. We waited for dawn. If you ask me why, I shall give the answer that my colleague, to whom I put the same question, gave me.

The murderer's first reflex, on hearing us, would undoubtedly have been to smash the gas burner in his room. We should thus have been in darkness, and he would have had an advantage over us.

'A man's resistance is always lower in the early morning,' Dufour told me, and I've confirmed this subsequently.

We crept into the passage. Everybody was asleep around us. Taking infinite care, Dufour turned the key in the lock.

As I was the tallest and the heaviest, it was my job to rush forward first, and I did so at one bound, and found myself on top of the man as he lay stretched out in bed, grabbing him by whatever I could get hold of.

I don't know how long the struggle went on, but it seemed to me interminable. I felt myself rolling on the ground with him. I could see a fierce face close to my own. I remember particularly a set of huge dazzling teeth. A hand, clutching my ear, was trying to wrench it off.

I was not conscious of what my colleague was doing, but I saw an expression of pain and rage on my opponent's face. I felt him gradually loosen his hold. When I was able to turn round, Inspector Dufour, sitting cross-legged on the floor, was holding one of the man's feet in his hand, and it looked as if he'd been giving it at least a double twist.

'Handcuffs,' he ordered.

I had already handcuffed less dangerous prisoners, such as refractory prostitutes. This was the first time I had carried out a forcible arrest, and the sound of handcuffs put an end for me to a fight which might have ended badly.

· · ·

When people talk about a detective's flair, or his methods, his intuition, I always want to retort :

'What about your cobbler's flair, or your pastrycook's?'

Both of these have gone through years of apprenticeship. Each of them knows his job and everything concerned with it.

The same is true of a man from Police Headquarters. And that's why all the stories I have read, including those of my friend Simenon, are more or less inaccurate.

We sit in our office, drawing up reports. For this is also part of the job, a fact too frequently forgotten. I might even say that we spend far more time over administrative papers than on actual investigations.

We are told that a middle-aged gentleman is in the waiting-room, looking very nervous and asking to speak to the Chief immediately. Needless to say, the Chief hasn't time to receive all the people that turn up and want a personal interview because their little problem, to them, is the only important one.

There is one word which recurs so often that it has become like a refrain, and the office boy recites it like a litany : 'A matter of life and death.'

'Are you seeing him, Maigret?'

There is a little room next to the Inspectors' office for such interviews as these.

'Sit down. Cigarette?'

More often than not, before the visitor has had time to tell us his profession and his social status we have guessed them.

'It's a very delicate matter, quite personal.'

A bank cashier, or an insurance agent, a man with a quiet regular way of life.

'Your daughter?'

It's either his son or his daughter or his wife. And we can foretell almost word for word the speech he's going to pour forth to us. No. His son hasn't taken money out of the boss's cash box. Nor has his wife gone off with a young man.

It's his daughter, a very well-brought-up young girl about whom there has never been a word of criticism. She saw nobody, lived at home and helped her mother with the housework.

Her girl friends were as serious-minded as herself. She practically never went out alone.

And yet she's vanished, taking some of her belongings with her.

What can you tell him? That six hundred people disappear every month in Paris and that about two-thirds of them are found?

'Is your daughter very pretty?'

He has brought several photographs, convinced that they'll be useful for our search. If she's pretty, so much the worse, for the number of chances is lessened. If she's ugly, on the contrary, she'll probably come back in a few days or a few weeks.

'You can rely on us. We'll do what's necessary.'

'When?'

'Right away.'

He's going to ring us up every day, twice a day, and there is nothing to tell him, except that we haven't had time to look for the young lady.

Almost always a brief enquiry reveals that a young man living in the same block of flats, or the grocer's assistant, or the brother of one of her girl friends has disappeared on the same day as herself.

You cannot go through Paris and France with a fine-tooth comb for a runaway girl, and her photograph will merely go next week to join the collection of prints sent to police stations, to the various branches of the force and to frontier posts.

.        .        .

Eleven o'clock at night. A telephone call from the Emergency Office, over the way, in the building of the Municipal Police, where all calls are centralised and inscribed on a luminous board that takes up the whole breadth of a wall.

The Pont de Flandre station has just heard that there's been trouble in a bar in the Rue de Crimée.

It's right the other side of Paris. Nowadays Headquarters has a few cars at its disposal, but formerly, you had to take a cab, or later a taxi, for which you couldn't be sure you'd be refunded.

The bar, at a street corner, is still open, with a broken window, figures standing prudently at some distance, for in that district people prefer not to attract the attention of the police.

Uniformed constables are there already, an ambulance, sometimes the Station Officer or his secretary.

On the ground, amidst the sawdust and spittle, a man lies crumpled up, one hand on his breast, from which a trickle of blood is flowing to form a pool.

'Dead!'

Beside him, on the floor, a small suitcase, which he was holding when he fell, has burst open, letting drop some pornographic postcards.

The anxious barkeeper tries to put himself in the right.

'Everything was quiet, as usual. This is a respectable house.'

'Had you seen him before?'

'Never.'

The answer was inevitable. He probably knows him very well, but he'll go on asserting to the end that it was the first time the man had set foot in his bar.

'What happened?'

The dead man is a drab figure, middle-aged or rather of indeterminate age. His clothes are old, of doubtful cleanliness, his shirt collar is black with grime.

Useless to hunt for relatives or a home. He must have been staying in the lowest type of furnished lodgings, on a weekly rate, and set off thence to hawk his wares in the neighbourhood of the Tuileries and the Palais-Royal.

'There were three or four customers...'

No point in asking where they are. They've flown away, and will not come back to give evidence.

'Did you know them?'

'Vaguely. By sight only.'

Of course! We could give his answers for him.

'A stranger came in and sat down at the other side of the bar, just opposite this chap.'

The bar is horseshoe-shaped, with overturned glasses on it and a strong smell of cheap spirits.

'They didn't speak to one another. This chap looked frightened. He put his hand into his pocket to pay . . .'

That is so, for he had no weapon on him.

'The other chap never said a word, but pulled out his gun and fired three times. He'd have gone on probably if his revolver hadn't jammed. Then he calmly pulled his hat down over his eyes and went out.'

That's clear enough. No need of flair. The *milieu* in which we have to hunt is a particularly restricted one.

There aren't so many of them who peddle dirty pictures. We know nearly all of them. Periodically they pass through our hands, serve a short sentence in gaol and then begin again.

The dead man's shoes – his feet are dirty and there are holes in his socks – bear the mark of a Berlin firm.

He is a newcomer. He must have been given the hint that there was no room for him in the district. Or else he was a subordinate to whom the goods were entrusted and who had kept the money for himself.

It'll take three days, four perhaps. Hardly longer. The Hotels Squad will promptly be called upon to help and, before the next night, will know where the victim was staying.

The Vice Squad, armed with his photograph, will pursue their separate enquiry.

This afternoon, in the neighbourhood of the Tuileries, they'll arrest some of those individuals who all offer passers-by the same trash with an air of mystery.

They won't be very nice to them. In the old days they were even less so than they are today.

'Have you ever seen that fellow?'

'No.'

'Are you sure you've never met him?'

There's a certain little cell, very dark, very narrow, a sort of cupboard rather, on the mezzanine floor, where people like that are helped to remember, and it seldom happens that after a few hours they don't start banging on the door.

'I think I've caught sight of him ...'

'His name?'

'I only know his first name : Otto.'

The skein will unwind slowly, but it will unwind to the end, like a tapeworm.

'He's a queer!'

Good! The fact that a homosexual is involved restricts the field of enquiry still further.

'Didn't he often go to the Rue de Bondy?'

It was almost inevitable. There's a certain little bar there frequented by practically all homosexuals of a certain social level – the lowest. There's another in the Rue de Lappe, which has become an attraction for sightseers.

'Whom have you seen him with?'

That's about all. It only remains, when we get the man between four walls, to make him confess and sign his confession.

.    .    .

All cases aren't as simple as that. Some investigations take months. And certain criminals are eventually arrested only after long years, and then sometimes by pure chance.

In practically every case, the process is the same.

You have to *know*.

To know the *milieu* in which a crime has been committed, to know the way of life, the habits, morals, reactions of the people involved in it, whether victims, criminals or merely witnesses.

To enter into their world without surprise, easily, and to speak its language naturally.

This is as true whether we are concerned with a bistro in La Villette or the Porte d'Italie, or with the Arabs in the Zone, with Poles or Italians, with the streetwalkers of Pigalle or the young delinquents of Les Ternes.

It's still true if we are concerned with the racing world or the gambling world, with safe-breaking specialists or jewel thieves.

That is why we aren't wasting our time when we spend years pacing the pavements, climbing stairs or spying on pilferers in big stores.

Like the cobbler, like the pastrycook, we are serving our apprenticeship, with this difference, that it goes on for practically the whole of our lives, because the number of different circles is almost infinite.

Prostitutes, pickpockets, cardsharpers, confidence tricksters or specialists in cheque forgery recognise one another.

One might say the same of policemen after a certain number of years on the job. And it's not a matter of hob-nailed shoes or moustaches.

I think it's the look in our eyes that gives us away, a certain reaction – or rather lack of reaction – when confronted with certain creatures, certain states of destitution, certain abnormalities.

With all due deference to novelists, a detective is, above all, a professional. He is an *official*.

He's not engaged in a guessing game, nor getting worked up over a relatively thrilling chase.

When he spends a night in the rain, watching a door that doesn't open or a lighted window, when he patiently scans the pavement cafés on the Boulevards for a familiar face, or prepares to spend hours questioning a pale, terrified individual, he is doing his daily job.

He is earning his living, trying to earn as honestly as possible the money that the Government gives him at the end of every month in remuneration for his services.

I know that my wife, when she reads these lines presently, will shake her head and look at me reproachfully, murmuring maybe:

'You always exaggerate!'

She will probably add:

'You're going to give a wrong idea of yourself and your colleagues.'

She's quite right. I may possibly be exaggerating somewhat in the contrary direction. It's by way of reaction against the ready-made ideas which have so often irritated me.

How many times, after the publication of one of Simenon's books, have my colleagues looked at me mockingly as I went into my office!

I could read in their eyes what they were thinking: 'Well, here comes God the Father!'

That is why I insist on the term official, which others consider derogatory.

I have been an official almost all my life. Thanks to Inspector Jacquemain, I became one on the threshold of manhood.

Just as my father, in his day, became estate manager at the château. With the same pride. With the same concern to know everything about my job and to carry out my task conscientiously.

The difference between other officials and those of the Quai des Orfèvres is that the latter are, as it were, balanced between two worlds.

By their dress, by their education, by their homes and their way of life, they are indistinguishable from other middle-class people and share their dream of a little house in the country.

Most of their time is spent none the less in contact with

the underworld, the riffraff, the dregs, often with the enemies of organised society.

This has often struck me. It's a strange situation about which I have sometimes felt uneasy.

I live in a bourgeois apartment, where the savoury smells of my carefully-prepared dinner await me, where everything is simple and neat, clean and comfortable. Through my windows I see only homes like my own, mothers walking with their children along the boulevard, housewives going to do their shopping.

I belong to that social group, of course, to what are known as respectable people.

But I know the others too, I know them well enough for a certain contact to exist between myself and them. The tarts at the Brasserie in the Place de la République, when I go by, know that I understand their language and the meaning of their attitudes. So does the street-arab threading his way through the crowd.

And all the others whom I have met and still meet every day, under the most intimate conditions.

Isn't this enough to make some sort of bond?

It's not my business to make excuses for them, to justify or absolve them. It's not my business, either, to adorn them with some sort of halo, as was the fashion at one time.

It's my business simply to consider them as a fact, to look at them with the eye of one who knows them.

Without curiosity, because curiosity is quickly dulled.

Without hatred, of course.

To look as them, in short, as creatures who exist and

who, for the well-being of society, for the sake of the established order, have got to be kept, willy nilly, within certain bounds and punished when they overstep them.

They are well aware of this themselves! They bear us no grudge for it. They often say :

'You're doing your job.'

As for what they think of that particular job, I'd rather not try to find out.

Is it surprising that after twenty-five or thirty years in the Force we walk with a rather heavy step, and have in our eyes an even heavier look, sometimes a blank look?

'Don't you sometimes feel disgusted?'

No, I don't! And it's probably through my job that I have acquired a fairly unshakeable optimism.

Paraphrasing a saying of my first religious instructor, I should like to say : a little knowledge turns one away from man, a great deal of knowledge brings one back to man.

It's because I have witnessed depravities of every sort that I have come to realise that they were compensated by a great deal of simple courage, good will or resignation.

Utterly rotten individuals are rare, and most of those I have come across, unfortunately, functioned out of my reach, out of our sphere of action.

As for the rest, I tried to prevent them from doing too much harm and to see to it that they paid for the harm they had already done.

After which, surely, we've settled our accounts.

That chapter is closed.

## CHAPTER EIGHT

*The Place des Vosges, a young lady's engagement and
some little notes from Madame Maigret.*

'ON the whole,' Louise said, 'I don't see all that much difference.'

I always look rather anxiously at her when she's reading what I have just been writing, trying to forestall her criticisms.

'Difference between what?'

'Between what you say about yourself and what Simenon says about you.'

'Oh!'

'Perhaps I'm wrong to give my opinion.'

'No, no, of course not!'

All the same, if she is right, I've given myself needless trouble. And it's quite possible that she is right, that I haven't known how to go about it, how to set things out as I had promised myself.

Or else the famous tirade about made-up truths being truer than naked truths is not a mere paradox.

I have done my best. Only there are heaps of things that struck me as essential at the beginning, points I had determined to develop and which I have abandoned on the way.

For instance, one shelf of the bookcase is full of Simenon's books, which I have patiently stuffed with blue pencil marks, and I was looking forward to correcting all the mistakes he's made, either because he didn't know, or else for the sake of picturesqueness, often because he hadn't the courage to ring me up to verify some detail.

What's the use? I should look like a fussy fellow, and I'm beginning to believe myself that these things are not so very important.

One of his habits that irritated me most sometimes was that of mixing up dates, of setting at the beginning of my career investigations that took place much later on, and vice versa, so that sometimes my detectives are described as being quite young, whereas they were really staid fathers of families at the period in question, or the other way round.

I had even thought seriously, I confess it now that I've given up the idea, of establishing, thanks to the files of newspaper cuttings which my wife has kept up to date, a chronology of the principal cases in which I've been involved.

'Why not?' Simenon replied. 'Excellent idea. They'll be able to correct my books for the next edition.'

He added, without irony:

'Only, Maigret old fellow, you'll have to be kind enough to do the job yourself, for I've never had the courage to re-read my own books.'

I have said what I had to say, on the whole, and it cannot be helped if I've said it badly. My colleagues will understand, and everyone who's more or less connected with the Force, and it's chiefly for them that I was anxious to put things right, to speak not so much of myself as of our profession.

It looks as if some important question had escaped me. I hear my wife carefully opening the door of the dining-room where I am working, and tiptoeing forward.

She has just put a scrap of paper on the table before withdrawing in the same fashion. I read these pencilled words :

'Place des Vosges.'

And I can't resist smiling with private satisfaction, for this proves that she too has details to put right, one at least, and, actually, for the same reason as myself, out of loyalty.

In her case it's out of loyalty to our flat in the Boulevard Richard-Lenoir, which we have never deserted, which still belongs to us today, although we only use it a few days a year, now that we're living in the country.

In several of his books Simenon described us as living in the Place des Vosges without offering the slightest explanation.

I'm giving my wife's message then. It's quite true that for a number of months we lived in the Place des Vosges. But we were not in our own home.

That year our landlord had at last decided to get the building refaced, which it had been needing for some time. In front of the house, workmen had set up scaffolding which surrounded our windows. Others, inside, began making holes in the walls and floor to instal central heating. We had been promised that it would take three weeks at most. After a fortnight they had got nowhere, and just at that time a strike was declared in the building trade and nobody knew how long it might last.

Simenon was just off for Africa, where he was to spend nearly a year.

'Why don't you move into my flat in the Place des Vosges until the job's finished?'

And so it happened that we went to live there, at No. 21 to be exact, without incurring the reproach of disloyalty to our dear old Boulevard.

There was one period, too, in which, without warning me, he made me retire when I still had several years' service to run.

We had just bought our house at Meung-sur-Loire and we used to spend all my free Sundays getting it ready. He came to visit us there. The place delighted him so much that in the next book he quite shamelessly anticipated events, made me several years older and settled me there for good.

'It makes a change of atmosphere,' he told me when I spoke to him about it. '*I was getting bored with the Quai des Orfèvres.*'

Allow me to underline that sentence, which seems to me outrageous. It's he, you notice, who was getting bored with the Quai, with my office, with the daily duties at Headquarters!

Which did not prevent him subsequently, and will probably not prevent him in future from relating earlier investigations, still giving no dates, making me sometimes sixty years old and sometimes forty-five.

Here's my wife again. I have no study at home. I don't need one. When I have to work I settle down at the dining-room table, and Louise retires into the kitchen, which she's quite glad to do. I look at her, thinking she wants to tell me something. But it's another scrap of paper which she's got in her hand and has come to lay timidly in front of me.

This time it's a list, just like when I'm going to town and she writes down on a scrap torn out of her notebook what I've got to bring her back.

My nephew heads the list, and I understand why. He's her sister's son. I got him into the Police force a long time ago, at an age when he was fired with enthusiasm about it.

Simenon mentioned him, then the boy suddenly disappeared from his books, and I can guess Louise's scruples. She's been thinking that for some readers this may have appeared suspicious, as though her nephew had committed some folly.

The truth is quite simple. He hadn't done as brilliantly as he had hoped. And he did not put up much resistance to his father-in-law's pressing offers of a place in his soap factory at Marseilles.

The name of Torrence comes next on the list, big noisy Torrence (I believe that somewhere or other Simenon makes him die in place of another detective who was in fact killed by my side in a Champs-Elysées hotel).

Torrence had no father-in-law in soap. But he had a

terrific appetite for life, together with a business sense that was hardly compatible with the existence of an official.

He left us to found a private detective agency, a highly respectable agency, I hasten to add, for that is not always the case. And for a long time he kept on coming to the Quai to ask for our help, or for information, or merely to breathe the atmosphere of the place again.

He has a big American car which stops from time to time in front of our door, and each time he is accompanied by a pretty woman, always a different one, whom he introduces with unvarying sincerity as his fiancée.

I read the third name, little Janvier as we have always called him. He is still at the Quai. Probably they still call him little Janvier?

In his last letter he informs me, not without a certain melancholy, that his daughter is engaged to a young man from the École Polytechnique.

Finally Lucas who, at the present moment, is probably sitting as usual in my office, at my desk, smoking one of my pipes which he begged me, with tears in his eyes, to leave him as a souvenir.

There's one word at the bottom of the list. I thought at first it was a name, but I couldn't decipher it.

I have just gone into the kitchen, where I was quite surprised to see bright sunlight, for I had closed the shutters in order to work in a half-light which I find helpful.

'Finished?'

'No. There's one word I can't read.'

She was quite embarrassed.

'It doesn't matter at all.'

'What is it?'

'Nothing. Don't pay any attention to it.'

Of course I insisted.

'Sloe gin!' she admitted at last, averting her head.

She knew I should burst out laughing, as in fact I did.

When it was a question of my famous bowler hat, my velvet-collared overcoat, my coal stove and my poker, I was well aware that she thought I was being childish when I insisted on making corrections.

Nevertheless she has herself scribbled the words *sloe gin* at the bottom of the list, making them illegible on purpose, I'm convinced, out of a sort of shame, rather like when she adds to the list of errands to be done in town some very feminine article which she rather shamefacedly asks me to buy for her.

Simenon has mentioned a certain bottle which we always had in our sideboard in the Boulevard Richard-Lenoir – we still have it there – and of which my sister-in-law, according to a hallowed tradition, brings us a supply from Alsace on her annual visit there.

He has thoughtlessly described it as sloe gin.

Actually it is raspberry brandy. And for an Alsatian, apparently, this makes a tremendous difference.

'I've made the correction, Louise. Your sister will be satisfied.'

This time I left the kitchen door open.

'Nothing else?'

'Tell the Simenons I'm knitting socks for . . .'

'But I'm not writing them a letter, you know!'

'Of course. Make a note of it for when you do write. They're not to forget the photo they promised us.'

She added:

'Can I lay the table?'

That's all.

Meung-sur-Loire, Sept. 27, 1950.